Grobar and the Mind Control Potion

Joseph J. Cox

Suckerfish Books
www.suckerfishbooks.com

This is a work of fiction. Everything is imaginary. Any resemblence to real people, businesses or geese is entirely coincidental. The two-legged water-bird in a trench coat who just walked by is only a figment of your imagination.

Suckerfish Books
23700 NW Skyline Blvd, North Plains, OR 97124

Suckerfish Books Australia
19 McGuiness Road, East Bentleigh, VIC, Australia 3165

Library of Congress Preassigned Control Number: 2005904086
ISBN: 0-9764659-3-0
13-digit ISBN: 978-0-9764659-3-5

Printed in the United States of America

Cover Art by
Rebecca J. Becker

ISBN 0-9764659-3-0

50995>

9 780976 465935

$9.95US

This book is dedicated to Mrs. Shaff,
who told me I had to be a famous author
before I could use 'But' at the beginning of a sentence.

I would also like to thank
my wife for her continual support,
my mom for her sharp editing,
my nephew Atniel for the title,
Rebecca J. Becker for a phenomenal cover,
and the countless readers (and critics)
who have helped make this book what it is.

(NARRATOR)

Thursday

Thursday's office was a low-rent hole in the ground. He was a hard working guy who didn't care much for luxury. He was more interested in keeping a low profile and getting his work done. Thursday was a spy, a secret agent, a spook. The less people noticed him, the better he could do his job.

Imaginary spies, like those you see in the movies, put themselves up at fancy hotels, and are surrounded by ferris wheels and fast cars.

But Thursday wasn't imaginary.

He believed in keeping his eyes on the ball. All that fancy stuff didn't do much for him. Some people might say that Thursday took 'low-profile' a little too far. When he went looking for office space, he didn't go to the low-rent district like some private detective from an old movie – no, he made his own low-rent district. He bought an old waterpark, got it fixed up, and in the process built himself a nice plastic bunker under the main pool. His bunker wasn't decked out with funky couches, a shark tank or any of that cool stuff. It just had his equipment, a small mat on the floor for sleeping, a little fridge for ice cream and old pizza with anchovies, and that was about it.

The place wasn't designed for guests. Which was why the pile on the floor that went by the name of Short Eddy was such a problem.

A few minutes earlier, Mean Eyes Paine and his gang of bullies had been trying to drown Short Eddy in the waterpark pool. Thursday had watched on his surveillance equipment, and he'd hoped that the bullies would let Short Eddy up for air. But they didn't. So, using a robotic arm disguised as an automatic pool cleaner, Thursday had dragged Eddy into the bunker's waterlock.

A moment after the waterlock had drained, Short Eddy opened the door and stumbled into Thursday's office.

The kid was sputtering, but he was breathing. He coughed a few times and then stood up straight and looked around the room. Thursday saw Short Eddy's brain trying to figure out what was going on.

Short Eddy stopped looking around when his eyes finally got around to Thursday. He looked at Thursday for about five seconds, his jaw slowly dropping lower and lower. Then, Short Eddy, the 4th grade nerd who always got pushed around at school, just passed out on the floor. He made a very unsatisfying thump as he landed.

It wasn't unexpected.

Thursday wasn't quite like most secret agents. He wasn't tall, he wasn't dashing and he didn't have the fastest hands in – well, he didn't have hands at all.

Nonetheless, he always looked great in a tux.

Thursday wasn't just a spy.

He was a penguin spy.

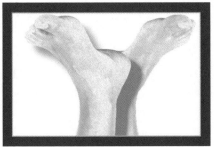

(SHORT EDDY)

Eddy

Okay, let's get one thing straight. I didn't faint because I was scared.
I fainted because the little guy I was faced with was so incredibly
funny.

A couple of minutes before I passed out, I'd been at the waterpark. I'd actually been playing in the pool. Well, maybe I wasn't
playing. It might be more accurate to say that I was being picked on
by the school bully – Mean Eyes Paine. Although now that I think
about it, I guess 'being picked on' might be a bit of an understatement. I was really being drowned. Mean Eyes Paine and his group of
thugs were, as far as I could tell, trying to kill me. They were even
videotaping it.

Thankfully, they failed.

They didn't fail due to a lack of firepower – there were ten of
them and they were all much bigger than me. And they didn't fail
because they didn't have the nerve to go through with it – they got
awful close to ending it all. They didn't even fail because some lifeguard suddenly showed up and saved me. No, they failed because,
just as I was beginning to drown, this thing grabbed my legs and
pulled me down into this little room under the pool.

3

Now, I'm about to tell you some pretty strange stuff. But, even though I may have been drowning, I wasn't hallucinating or anything. Everything I'm about to tell you is perfectly true.

The little room under the pool, the one the arm dragged me to, had one major problem. It was filled to the brim with water. Just then, I wasn't feeling all that lucky. At least I'd had a *chance* with Mean Eyes Paine.

I was about to give up when, suddenly, the water in the room drained.

I was very relieved.

Then another door opened. Thankfully, this door didn't lead up to the pool. That would have been bad. I was sure Mean Eyes Paine was waiting for me. Instead, the door led into this weird office.

Now before you get this picture of a nice room with Venetian blinds, secretaries, cubicles and fluorescent lighting let me tell you that this office had none of that. Well, it did have fluorescent lighting, but that was probably just to save on the electricity bill.

The weirdest thing about the room was that it looked like it was made out of waterslide plastic. The plastic lent a really strange blue glow to the room. The other really weird thing was that there wasn't a flat spot in the entire room. All the corners were curved like some waterslide tube. The room was full of lots and lots of really cool equipment. I didn't know what it all was, but that didn't stop me from thinking it was pretty cool.

So I'm looking at all this stuff and I'm pretty confused. I mean, I hadn't been expecting any of it. And then, I saw him.

Standing, right in the middle of the room, was a penguin. A penguin! I don't live in Antarctica or anything. I live in Lakedale, USA and we don't have penguins. Not even at the aquarium. Naturally, I was pretty surprised to find myself face-to-face – or to be more accurate leg-to-face with a little water-bird.

I wasn't scared though.

4

I just thought it was funny. Now, you might ask, 'What's so funny about a penguin?' Well, this wasn't any normal penguin. This bird was wearing a tuxedo, carrying a blow gun, and strutting around like he was some kind of secret agent. When you picture it, you'll understand that it was just too much to take. So, I fell over laughing. Unfortunately, I hit my head on something and passed out. It's that simple.

If the penguin tells you any different, he's lying.

When I woke up, the penguin was standing next to my head. You have to remember that when I'm lying down and he's standing up, his beak isn't much higher than the tip of my nose. After all, he's only a foot tall. So this penguin was standing there, looking at me and then, get this, he tried to scare me. He was eating from this little bowl of ice cream like that was the coolest thing a penguin could do. And then he glowered at me with his little penguin eyes, he shook his little penguin wings, and he said, in perfect English, "What shall we do with you?"

I almost fainted again.

I mean, here's this little guy, cute as can be. I could have picked him up and thrown him across the room, and he's looking all mean and he's threatening me. I tried very very hard not to giggle.

Then, I decided to get up. And you know what? While I was asleep, the penguin had tied me down. I couldn't move. Then, the little guy pulls out a mean-looking syringe. And he says, "You think you can pick me up and throw me across the room."

It wasn't a question, but I kinda nodded anyways, not really sure if he was asking whether I could do it normally, or tied down like I was. He ate a little bit of his ice cream and then said, "Lots of people underestimate penguins."

I could see what he meant. I certainly hadn't expected to be tied down and faced with a syringe full of some unknown substance. I mean, the guy was a foot tall and he didn't even have hands. And then he asked the strangest question of all, "*Who* sent you?"

Who sent me? Nobody sent me. Except maybe Mean Eyes Paine. Mean Eyes and his pals had been trying to drown me in the pool. Whatever Mean Eyes Paine had been trying, he certainly hadn't meant me to end up in this penguin's lair. I guess that was the closest answer to what he wanted, so I said, "Mean Eyes Paine sent me."

He looked at me real close – if I could have moved my neck I could have bit his nose off. He breathed cold ice cream air into my face (and yes, it gave me a bit of a headache) and he said, "You work for Mean Eyes Paine?"

And I said, "I hate the guy."

His little eyes bored into me, "We can do this the easy way or the hard way. Do you work for him?"

And I said, spelling out each of the words clearly, "No, I do not."

It sounded like the answer he wanted to hear because he suddenly brightened up and said, "Thank you."

Then, in a completely flat voice he said, "Now, I'm going to give you a shot. And after you receive it, you aren't going to remember any of this. When you wake up, the waterpark lifeguard will be pulling you from the pool. And then your life will go on like you'd never met me."

I'm telling you this story, so obviously his plan didn't work so well. I mean, if it had, I wouldn't know about him, right? So doubtless, you're curious about what happened. Well, I didn't want to forget anything that had happened and I was real curious to learn even more. I'll admit, I also didn't want him to stick me with his needle. I don't like needles. So, to make a short story finally end, I decided to ask him a few questions of my own.

6

I said, "That sounds like a good idea, Mr. Penguin. My mom is probably worrying about me and it'd be best for me to get back soon. I mean, we're having fish for dinner and I wouldn't want to miss out on that. But I have one question, being as you are going to make me forget everything, can you tell me what you do?"

What I said wasn't entirely true. I mean, my mom was waiting for me, but she was waiting at home. We live right around the corner from the water park, so I go there all the time. She didn't expect me back for a few hours and certainly wouldn't miss me until then. I go out lots. It's just what I do.

He thought for a moment, as if considering, and then he took the bait. "My name's Thursday," he said, "I'm a secret agent – a secret agent penguin. People don't know much about us because we work in the shadows, but we protect people like you from some of the tyrants, dictators and murderers roaming the planet earth."

(I would have laughed if he hadn't tied me down. I mean, I could have laughed, but I didn't because you tend to take foot-tall creatures who can tie you down really seriously.)

"I am based in Lakedale because, unbeknownst to you, Lakedale is a nexus of information. All that's happening in America – and sometimes beyond – crosses through your strip malls, grocery stores and leafy playgrounds. I am here; I listen, and occasionally, I act."

"Unbeknownst to me?" I interjected. "What do you mean unbeknownst to me? I know everything that's going on in this town!" I was bluffing, but I thought I might be able to pull it off.

"Oh," challenged Thursday, "did you know Mr. Frank at the pharmacy deals in forged passports?"

"Ha!" I said. "Of course I know. But did you know that he doesn't actually make them himself?" I had actually seen Mr. Frank buying passports, or something like them, from a man in his store.

As I expected, Thursday seemed genuinely surprised. He took another nibble of his ice cream. Then he put it and his syringe down. He pulled out a little notebook and a little pen and asked, "Who makes them?"

I wasn't about to tell him. After all, I didn't even know and I had to string him along to find out what would make him let me go. And I had an idea where to start. The penguin, Thursday, needed information. I didn't have any, but I might just be able to convince him that I did. Maybe, just maybe, I could get him to let me in on the action. I wanted to go on a secret mission. I figured I might be able to get away with that if I played my cards right.

So I said, "I'm not going to tell you."

"Not going to tell me?" he said. "The fate of the free world hangs in the balance and you're going to keep your secrets from me?"

His voice was completely monotone. It was eerie.

"What? Me keep my secrets from you! You were about to stick me with some goopy stuff to keep your identity and very existence secret from me and now you want me to tell you everything?"

"Yes, I want you to tell me everything. I'm a secret agent. I've been highly trained by the most advanced spy training academy in the world located in Penguin City. I am qualified to use your information and you are not qualified to even know about me. So tell me your secrets."

"No," I said. "I don't even know that you're a good guy. You might work for the bad guys and telling you secrets might be the stupidest thing I'll ever do."

Thursday looked at me, considered me carefully and then said, very slowly, "Don't repeat a word about me to anybody. I'll let you go without giving you the forgetting drug. It will give you, and me, some time to think. We might be able to help each other out."

"What if my mom asks why I'm late for dinner?" I said.

"If your mom asks, then you can tell her. But nobody else," the little bird responded, sternly. With the flick of a switch, my bonds were released. I stood up and looked down at the little bird. He pointed out the door with his wing. I thought about picking him up, but chances were he had considered the possibility. So, I turned, and walked through the door and back into the little room I had come through. A computerized voice said, "Hold your breath."

I held my breath.

A moment later, the ceiling disappeared and a massive gush of water filled the room. I shot upwards. When my head popped out of the water, I was back in the waterpark pool.

(NARRATOR)

Grobar

The house Grobar grew up in wasn't very big. Actually, it had only one room. The entire family lived in that one room. The room had two beds. One for the parents, and one for the kids. The memories of that house were the happiest of Grobar's life.

Growing up, Grobar would gently fall asleep, a bottle in his mouth, a smile on his face, and a story in his mind. He slept right there, curled up next to Ulu, his big brother. Grobar knew he was adopted, but he had always felt like a real member of the family. Especially around Ulu. He and Ulu spent the days playing and the evenings listening to stories about far-away lands. They spent all their time together. They were not only brothers, they were best friends.

Grobar remembered, extremely clearly, the day his family decided to move from the prairie to the city. For months, they had planned it. They saved money, they packed up their belongings and they thought about the future. While everybody was excited, Grobar was the most excited of all. He'd never seen a city, so all he could do was listen to the pictures painted by Ulu and his parents. In the city, things were busy, stuff was going on, buildings were crammed right up next to each other. It was so strange to Grobar that he could barely imagine it. But it didn't stop him from dreaming. Night after night, he dreamt of life in the city.

Sadly, it wasn't to be. When moving day came, Grobar discovered that he wasn't invited. Of course, the family wasn't just going to abandon him. No, instead they decided to give him away. Ulu, to his credit, did put up a fight. He started screaming and crying that he didn't want to leave Grobar behind. "WHY?" he shouted, his voice full of pain, "WHY CAN'T GROBAR COME WITH US?"

His mother only had one answer, "Dear Ulu," she said, softly brushing the tears off of his face, "Grobar can't come because he's not a real member of the family. He's just a goat."

When he heard those words, Grobar's heart almost stopped. It had never occurred to him before that the family he'd loved would think that he was "just a goat." Heartbroken, Grobar didn't want to be given away and he didn't wait for a goodbye hug from Ulu. Instead, he simply turned around and walked away, never to return.

Grobar didn't starve when he left home. He didn't move in with anybody else either. Instead, he wandered the countryside for years. He found himself a new home and he learned about the world by talking to the creatures of the prairie. But no matter how nice his house was, and no matter how much he learned, he realized that he wasn't getting any closer to his real goal.

He wasn't any closer to being happy.

And then, one day, while munching on some grass in the middle of nowhere, Grobar realized what he needed to do.

He needed to take over the world.

It was simple. His parents had thought he was "just a goat." Well, he decided, he'd show them.

And just like that, Grobar had a real purpose in life. He threw himself into his new project. He was no longer an innocent baby goat sucking on a bottle. No. Now he was Grobar the grown-up goat. He no longer aimlessly wandered the prairies. Now he stayed at home and planned. Somehow, at some point, he was going to come up with something that would make everything right.

He was curled up on the floor, hard at thought, when it finally hit him. Grobar stood up as straight as a goat can and exclaimed, "Ah ha! I've got it."

And because goats can't type, he proceeded to dictate *the entire plan* to his computer. His goal was in sight. He smiled the biggest smile he'd smiled in years.

Amidst the noise and excitement, he never noticed the small frog watching everything from a nearby table. He never noticed Bartholomew the Frog with Precision Hopping Ability.

(SHORT EDDY)

Home Sweet Home

As soon as I left the water park I went home. My mom was there, making dinner. As I walked in, she asked, "Edward, how was your day?"

I kinda mumbled, "Fine, Mom."

I wasn't trying to give away Thursday's secrets. But then she said, "Did anything interesting happen today?"

What was I supposed to do? She's my mom and she asked me a question. I couldn't just lie to her. So I told her about Thursday. The whole story – from Mark Paine trying to drown me, to me ending up in Thursday's lair, to my conversation with Thursday – it all came gushing out.

And do you know what she said? She said, "That's nice dear." Then she got out a little notebook and made a few notes and went back to cooking.

I got my hands on that notebook a little while later and do you know what it said? "Edward is compensating for being persecuted by a larger child by making up another imaginary story."

Another imaginary story? I know my mom doesn't believe my stories, and I know most of you don't believe my stories, but they aren't made up. I don't have some sort of fundamental problem that makes me think my stuffed tiger is real or something. Thursday was REAL. But my mom wouldn't have begun to believe that.

Despite my mom not believing me, she's a really cool character. My dad disappeared when I was about five and my mom has taken care of me ever since. She's done a really really good job too. Sometimes I worried about the situations I found myself in because I knew things like talking to spy penguins really unnerved her. She worries about me all the time and the encounters I had just made the situation worse. The amazing thing is that she still took it pretty much all in stride. She didn't break down and cry when I talked about Thursday, she just made little notes in a notebook. I thought it was a pretty good way of coping. Sometimes, I wished that could I stop upsetting her. After all, I love her and I never wanted to hurt her.

My mom and I live in a really cool house. The downstairs is all normal and stuff. We have a nice living room and a nice kitchen and a nice entryway. The upstairs is where the fun begins. My mom's room is pretty normal, but mine is something else again. First off, I can't even get into my room without thumbprint, voice and facial identification. The entire room is controlled by an advanced computer system that did all sorts of things, including controlling the door. To get in I have to put my thumb on a little pad next to the door, look at the handle and then say, "My name is Edward." The system thinks for a bit, and then if it all matches up, the door would swing open and the computer would say, "Welcome home, Edward."

I'm the only one it lets in, although I could program it to let other people in too.

Of course, I didn't design the system; my dad did – before he disappeared. He did a few cool things for me. Designing the door was one. A second was giving me what my dad called the Gryffin. I think he did at least. So, that was the name I'd always called it, even though I didn't know what it did. I did know that it was an almost perfectly black sphere which was a foot and a half tall and hovered in the air while expanding and contracting a little bit, like it was breathing. It was pretty weird looking. It was also very mysterious. Last but not least, it was also very, very important to my dad. It was so important that before he disappeared, my dad even gave me a picture of me and him with the Gryffin. I carried that picture everywhere – even the water park. It is in a special waterproof wrapper and it stays in my back pocket – no matter what.

The Gryffin itself lived in my room. It had its own table that I made with my mom's help. It also had its own light. So it sat there, for years, hovering above the table, with its very own light cast on it. It was kinda beautiful. I don't know why, but whenever I looked at it, it reminded me of my dad. I hoped my dad would show up sometime and show me how to use it. But he'd disappeared before I could learn more.

As much as I worried about my mom, I really missed my dad. I knew him disappearing was very very hard on my mom too. When I mentioned it, she would get this fiery glow in her eyes. It scared me a bit. So I didn't talk about it much.

My mom could be pretty strict about some things. For example, every night I had to do the same routine. First, even when I didn't have school, I had to do my homework. It didn't normally take very long, although I do have to admit that English and grammar were a bit slow for me – I've been told I'm not very good with dashes and I am always starting sentences with the wrong words. Otherwise, it was all pretty simple stuff. Math was my favorite. The next thing I had to do was eat dinner. The day I met Thursday, my mom had made some chicken with rice and some ugly looking vegetables. She had used both mushrooms and eggplant – I hate both. But dinner

15

was dinner and she wasn't going to let me eat anything else – or any-place else. Once dinner was done, my mom and I would usually play a game. She called it "spending quality time together." It wasn't very high quality if you ask me. We just sat there and played without talking much. We talked more when she was making dinner and I was running around the kitchen grabbing things for her. Nonetheless, we would always play a game. That night it was crib-bage. Finally, at long last, after the homework, the dinner and the game, I rushed back upstairs. You see, it wasn't going to be a com-pletely normal night. Most nights I'd just go to sleep, after every-thing my mom had me do, but that night I was going to do something completely different.

That night, I was going to follow Thursday.

Bartholomew

Bartholomew wasn't always Bartholomew the Frog with Precision Hopping Ability. Yes, he had always been Bartholomew the Frog. But the Precision Hopping Ability came later. When he was growing up, Bartholomew had no idea that he was anything other than an athletic frog. He always won at races. But he – like everybody around him – thought it was some extraordinary natural athletic ability. It was extraordinary. In fact, Bartholomew could run faster than the eye could see. First he was in one place, and then he was in another. It was stunning. By grade-school, Bartholomew was the national track and field champion. By middle-school, he was the world champion in the 100 meter, the 1/4 mile and the marathon – and the only reason it took him so long to claim those championships was that they had age restrictions. If you had ever flipped on ISSN (Inter-Species Sports Network, a restricted channel), you'd have known Bartholomew's smiling face perfectly.

While Bartholomew didn't compete with non-frogs, he was still the King of Hop. And he was still a kid.

Bartholomew was the most popular kid at his school. Everybody wanted to be like him. Everybody wanted to hang out with him. However, he only wanted to hang out with two people: Sam the Elephant and Subway the Ferret. They were his best friends. Sam was an elephant with dreams while Subway was a cadet in the Ferret Legion. Subway amazed Bartholomew. Subway already knew exactly what he was going to do when he grew up. Bartholomew had no idea. After all, how many times could he win every championship before it got boring? But Subway was never going to be bored. No, Subway was going to be a soldier in the Ferret Legion. Bartholomew couldn't really understand it. He'd asked Subway once, "Why are you going to risk your life in the Ferret Legion? Why not do something safer?" He always remembered Subway's answer. "Because, Bart," Subway said, carefully, "some things are worth the risk."

Bartholomew may have remembered the answer, but that didn't mean that he understood it.

By high-school Bartholomew was an international celebrity who raced not only against other frogs but even against other species. He was a record breaker in every race he ran. He even landed a job as an actor in beverage commercials. He was living high on the bog, so to speak.

Everything was going great.

Then, everything changed.

One day, Bartholomew realized that maybe he wasn't actually running. Maybe, he thought, he didn't see the terrain go by, because no terrain was actually going by. Maybe, he thought, no one could see him running by, because he never was.

Bartholomew didn't just wake up one day and start asking these questions. No, everything had seemed normal to him until the day he ran a marathon (and won) without even breaking the piece of ribbon at the end. Somehow, he crossed the finish line without crossing the finish line.

After the race, Bartholomew tried hopping from where he was to another continent. And he got there – immediately. And then he realized that his speed had nothing to do with athletics and everything to do with an incredible, and incredibly strange, talent.

18

Curious, Bartholomew kept trying different hops. He quickly realized that he could hop anywhere, precisely and instantly. Thus the name Bartholomew the Frog with Precision Hopping Ability. He could be sitting next to you and then in one hop be on the top of the Eiffel Tower. If you happen to be reading this book on top of the Eiffel Tower, then he could in one hop be on the capital dome in Washington, DC. Bartholomew could hop anywhere, instantly, and with great precision. He could hop to the top of the tallest mountain on the moon – although he wouldn't live very long if he tried. Or, he could hop to the 7-Eleven on Franklin Road in Boise, Idaho to pick up a frog-sized slurpie (he did this a lot, since it is the only 7-Eleven in the world that serves frog-sized slurpies, and Bartholomew liked slurpies).

His talent did have limitations though. First, Bartholomew couldn't hop to anyplace that didn't currently exist. He couldn't hop to where 'the Adams School used to be' or to where 'the Adams School is going to be.' Second, he couldn't hop anywhere relative to his current location. In other words, he couldn't hop to the 'nearest' anything, or to the 'farthest' anything, or to the 7-Eleven four miles away. The only way he could hop to someplace in relation to where he was already, was the old fashioned way – a few inches at a time.

Bartholomew, being a good frog, and an honest competitor, realized that his discovery meant the end of his athletic career. His hopping ability made the races unfair. Others were working hard to beat him, and they never stood a chance. Quietly, as quietly as an international competitor who holds every running record in history possibly could, Bartholomew retired. People wrote articles about how he was retiring in his prime because he wanted to be remembered as the fastest frog in the world. They said he didn't want to go into that slow decline that so many athletes experience. Of course,

Bartholomew knew better. He was never going to get slower, and that was exactly the problem. He thought about telling the press this, but they probably wouldn't have believed him – so he just let them live with their illusions.

Bartholomew did tell his two best friends what he really was. It occurred to him that he might be able to help Subway with his work. After all, Subway was now an enlisted Ferret and could probably use another set of eyes to help him out. To Bartholomew it was kind of a game. He'd hop ahead of a group of Ferrets on a mission and then he'd secretly hop back to Subway and tell him what to expect. It was really quite a bit of fun.

Then, one day, a mission went horribly wrong. Bartholomew could do nothing but watch as Subway and his platoon were ambushed. After a brutal assault, the enemy had left the ferrets behind to die. Bartholomew hopped right up next to his dying friend. With his little arms, he gently lifted Subway's head. He was nearing tears.

The dying ferret, Bartholomew's very best friend, looked up at him, a pained smile on his face, and said, "Bart, you've been a great friend."

And that was it.

That scene never left Bartholomew's mind. For years, he agonized over what went wrong. He dropped out of school and began drifting. It doesn't take long to drift if you can be anywhere, instantly. But drift he did, aimlessly. His life lacked purpose or direction. All night and all day he did only one thing, he dreamt about how he might have been able to help save Subway's life. He blamed himself for what went wrong. Perhaps, somehow, he could have detected the ambush earlier. Maybe he could have convinced Subway not to go on that particular mission. Perhaps, just maybe, he could have fought off the enemy. In reality, there was nothing Bartholomew could have done. No matter how much he agonized, no matter how many scenarios he dreamed of, nothing would ever bring Subway back.

Bartholomew was a very unhappy frog.

And then he met someone. No, not a girl frog, a human – Eddy's dad actually. Eddy's dad told Bartholomew what he had to do. He told Bartholomew that he had to follow in Subway's footsteps. Bartholomew had to use his special talent to carry on Subway's lifelong mission to improve the world.

In short, Bartholomew had to become a spy.

Secretly, with the advice of Eddy's dad, Bartholomew transformed himself. Everybody knew Bartholomew the Frog. He was a famous frog who was featured on "What ever happened to..." shows. Everybody knew his prime had passed and that he'd spent years drifting and now spent most of his time at home eating chocolate ladybugs, drinking SodaCo Cola and watching TV. They also knew that he still had the occasional gig as a advertising spokesman. What they didn't know – in fact, what nobody aside from Eddy's dad and Sam the Elephant knew – was that he had become 'The Source.'

Who was 'The Source?'

'The Source' was a spy extraordinaire. Spies like Thursday imagined Bartholomew in a trench coat furtively speaking with networks of informants and somehow pulling the world's secrets out of the ether of rumor and suspicion.

Bartholomew was nothing like that. He just hopped places, watched what was going on, and then left.

Every week since becoming 'The Source,' Bartholomew had done a routine hop. He would try to hop to 'where a mastermind has a plot to take over the world.' Most of the time he did those hops, nothing happened – after all, masterminds don't always have plots to take over the world. It did work on occasion though. That was how he found Grobar and overheard his plot.

Bartholomew's approach did have one major drawback. He could hop to 'where a mastermind has a plot to take over the world,' but he couldn't tell anybody else *where* that evil mastermind was. As far as Bartholomew knew, Grobar could have been beneath the deserts of Africa or in a secret bunker hidden below the peak of Mount Everest.

After watching Grobar dictate his plan, Bartholomew the Frog with Precision Hopping Ability thought long and hard about it. He knew it was a very, very good plan. For Bartholomew the question was just how good. If it was just a very, very good plan, then it probably wouldn't work. Most attempts to take over the world fail totally. Of course, if it was a very, very, *very* good plan then it just might succeed. And that changed everything.

Bartholomew realized that Grobar's plan just happened to be a very, very, *very* good plan. So, Grobar had to be stopped. Being 'The Source,' Bartholomew didn't just hop up to the people who could fix everything. He couldn't risk it. If some evil mastermind found out that he had to look for a little green frog while planning to take over the world, then that mastermind might know enough to stop that frog.

So who did Bartholomew turn to in cases like these? Who did he turn to when he knew of an evil plot that was so very good that it threatened the entire planet? Who did he tell when he wanted the information to fall into the hands of those who could do something about it?

He told none other than Sam the Elephant.

(SHORT EDDY)

On a Penguin's Tail

Why was I, a ten-year-old kid, going to follow Thursday? It's a good question, but it's still an easy one to answer. You see, I liked spying. I liked to read spy books. I liked to sneak around. I liked to play with gadgets. But, well, I'd never ever actually met a spy – at least until that day. I decided to follow Thursday because I wanted to be a spy. I also wanted to change the world – and I figured that spies got to do that in the very coolest ways.

So, as soon as I got upstairs, I grabbed my binoculars from my dresser, opened the window to my room and crawled out onto the awning. Once there, I grabbed the tree branch and shimmied along it to the trunk. Then, using a ladder I had built into the tree out of nailed pieces of wood, I climbed down to the ground. Waiting at the base of my tree was my bicycle. I hopped on it and sped over to the water park. It was getting pretty dark, but I knew the way really well. Plus, it wasn't far to go.

The whole situation might seem strange to you. How many ten-year-olds do you know who sneak out alone at night?

Well, I wasn't a completely normal kid. I tended to take these little trips. I used to ask for my mom's permission, but she always gave it. I thought she assumed I was out playing with other kids. I guessed she thought that would have been good for me. I used to tell

23

her that I went out exploring the city. I told her about things that I found. But she didn't listen, she just wrote in her little notebook and said that I could go out as long as I did my homework and ate dinner first. I didn't think she believed my stories. I thought she thought I was just making them up. For certain, I knew she didn't think I would be trailing secret agent penguins. If you were her, that wouldn't have been at the top of your list, would it?

In any case, when I got to the water park, I parked my bike in some trees. I was hidden really well when I stopped and pulled out my binoculars. I had a great spot from which to spy on Thursday. From where I was, I could see the water park entrance and even the pool above Thursday's lair. I was watching the water carefully when this huge out of focus penguin suddenly popped into my field of vision. Thursday wasn't anywhere near the pool, he was standing right in front of me.

I slowly and quietly put down the binoculars. Thursday was just ten feet away. He must have had some sort of tunnel that led underneath the water park entrance and, quite by accident, popped out right in front of me. Thursday was staying low to the ground. I'm not sure it was entirely out of choice. Foot-tall water-birds aren't great at towering above the landscape. Thursday's little trench coat made him almost invisible against the pavement of the sidewalk. But I saw him nonetheless. I felt pretty good about it. I was pretty sharp. I was tracking a real spy and he didn't even know it, near as I could tell.

But Thursday did seem awful cautious. Wherever he was going, it must have been pretty important. I almost jumped back when, all of a sudden, Thursday shoved himself flat against a wall, disappearing into the shadows. I looked around nervously before I saw some woman hurry by. She didn't see either of us. But she might have seen Thursday if he hadn't hidden.

Thursday emerged from the shadows and pulled a small device out of his pocket. With a touch of a button, the coolest little miniature car appeared. Thursday hopped in and hit the gas. Just like that, the penguin was on the move! I jumped on my bicycle and pedaled as fast as I possibly could. The thing was, Thursday was a fast driver. I was following him north. He was heading straight downtown. I knew roughly where he was going, but I just couldn't keep up. Thursday's car was just too fast for me. No matter how fast I pedaled, he just got farther and farther away. Eventually I couldn't see him any more at all.

I kept biking, hoping I'd catch up eventually. But, at least for now, Thursday was gone.

Finally, I got to downtown. It was farther than I normally went on my trips out of the house. But it wasn't like it was the farthest I'd ever been. I really like exploring. I knew downtown very well. I'd almost never been there during the daytime. But as it was nighttime, I knew what I'd see when I got there – empty sidewalks that ran between tall, dark, office buildings. The people who worked there had long since gone home. I biked down the main roads, hoping to encounter the penguin. But I didn't see him anywhere. Eventually, I got to the riverfront.

Lakedale has a very nice riverfront. There are parks on either side of the river. They are called Riverfront Park South (on the side I was on) and Riverfront Park North (on the other side). Both parks, but especially Riverfront Park South, have water fountains and trees all over the place. It is a really neat place. During the daytime, people bring their kids there and they run through the water fountains. Sometimes there are carnivals. Being nighttime, there weren't any kids around. But there were a few couples here and there, holding hands and looking out over the river. I was looking for the penguin and didn't have time to wonder why they did that. As it was, I was happy the couples were just walking around and were completely ignoring me. I was a spy; I didn't need any additional attention.

The riverfront seemed like just the kind of place where Thursday would be. I biked slowly; my eyes peeled looking for anything unusual. And then, in the distance, I saw him. Along the riverfront wall, there was a tiny figure. He was standing there, looking down towards the river. I couldn't make out what he was doing, but I did know one thing.

The little guy hadn't escaped me.

(NARRATOR)

The Meeting

Before Thursday had even left the waterpark, he'd sensed that somebody – or something – was following him. Most nights, just a suspicion would have been enough for him to pack it in and hit the sack.
Spies are very cautious; it tends to lengthen their careers. The
problem was, it wasn't most nights. Thursday wasn't going to meet
just anybody. He was going to meet Sam the Elephant. And he
wasn't just going to meet Sam the Elephant. He was going to meet
Sam the Elephant when Sam the Elephant had something very, very
important to tell him.

In an earlier phone call, Sam had informed Thursday that the
'The Source' had a story to spill. Any cadet out of PENGUIN
Academy knew that when 'The Source' has a story to spill, you don't
cancel the meeting because you feel a little uneasy. Thursday, and
spies like him, saw 'The Source' like hamburgers see prime rib. Sure,
Thursday knew he was good, but 'The Source' was delicious.

He had to go to the meeting.

But that didn't mean he had to be stupid about it. He wasn't just
going to waltz over to Sam wearing a strobe light and shouting at the
top of his lungs. No, he was going to make himself as invisible as he
possibly could. Being invisible wasn't something you just did. It

wasn't a simple matter of hitting a switch and disappearing. Being invisible takes tools and techniques. The art of invisibility is what separates a great spy from a dead one. And Thursday was a great spy.

He could stick to the shadows like the shadows stick to people. Thursday started by donning his special issue trench coat. It was pitch black. At night, it was almost impossible to see. Color wasn't the trench coat's only feature. It also masked his body heat and lowered his radar signature.

Thursday didn't stop there. He wanted to make *sure* he wasn't spotted. He didn't just walk out of the waterpark, he used a special tunnel that led straight from his office to a discrete location outside the waterpark grounds.

Clad in black, Thursday emerged from his tunnel. As he scanned his surroundings, he immediately saw where his uneasiness had been coming from. He *was* being followed. By Short Eddy. The kid was looking straight at him.

He shouldn't have expected anything less.

When Eddy passed out in Thursday's office, a photo had fallen out of his pants' pocket. It was a photo of a man Thursday had known very well, and of a device called the Gryffin. There was also a small kid in the picture. He looked like a baby version of Eddy. But Thursday wasn't sure – the photo could have been a plant. So Thursday questioned Eddy fiercely. And once he was satisfied that Eddy wasn't a plant, he knew he couldn't give Eddy the forgetting drug. Occasionally, the forgetting drug makes the recipient forget too much. And if Eddy was related to the man in the picture, he was too important to drug. On the other hand, Thursday hadn't wanted Eddy to tell everybody about the talking penguin. That's why he scared him just a bit. But he didn't want to hurt the kid. And he didn't want him to feel like an idiot.

So, when Thursday came out of the tunnel and saw Short Eddy, he pretended not to notice. And Eddy fell for it.

Thursday almost got caught by someone else though. As he was ignoring Eddy he almost got flattened by some woman who'd been hurrying by. Thankfully, she hadn't seen him.

Smoothly, Thursday pulled out his remote car caller and pressed the button. When his car pulled up, he got in and took off. His eyes on his rearview mirror, he saw Eddy get on his bicycle.

At first, Thursday drove slowly to let Eddy think he could keep up. He didn't want to disappoint the kid too quickly. But he didn't want Eddy to know about his meeting either. Like anybody else, Short Eddy was going to have to work his way up the ranks.

As Eddy pedaled hard, Thursday made sure he kept going just a little bit faster. Eventually, when he looked in his rearview mirror, he couldn't see Eddy at all. That was when he hit the gas. He didn't want to be late for the meeting.

Thursday enjoyed almost everything about the spy business. But nothing beat a good secret meeting with Sam the Elephant. Sam and Thursday – well actually Sam and everybody – just seemed to get along great. Thursday had first met Sam years earlier when Sam had been a (relatively) little elephant at the zoo. Sam didn't much care for the zoo, and Thursday knew it. So Thursday had helped him run away. Sam had never known that Thursday had helped him. But he was there, and he did. After Sam escaped, Thursday found him a good job crushing cars. He also made sure Sam had a steady supply of exotic nuts. In short, he made sure that Sam was taken care of. It was the least he could do for a friend.

What Thursday hadn't expected was that Sam would become involved in the spy business. One of the reasons Thursday enjoyed the meetings with Sam so much was that Sam had so little in common with most people in the spy business. He wasn't dark or sleuthy or secretive. He was a big friendly guy who couldn't hide behind a small house. He was the kind of guy you could imagine hanging out eating a sundae, every day, all day. He was the kind of guy you'd imagine getting picked on and pushed around by the kids at school. Well, you could imagine him getting picked on at school if you ignored for a moment that he weighed more than most monster trucks. But no matter how hard he tried, Thursday couldn't imagine how this big friendly guy knew 'The Source.'

Thursday never would have told anyone, but he dreamed of actually getting to meet the 'The Source' himself. Not in Lakedale, of course, but at some dark restaurant in a back alley of some mysterious European city.

Thursday didn't know Bartholomew. But Bartholomew knew Thursday perfectly. In fact, just to make sure things went smoothly, Bartholomew had followed Thursday – hopping from rooftop to rooftop – all the way from the waterpark to the riverfront. When Thursday got to the river, Bartholomew was already there, watching to make sure things went well. Bartholomew had learned from experience that in the spy business it always pays to be careful. Nonetheless, for all the possibilities Bartholomew had taken into account, not one of them had come close to considering the possibility that Short Eddy might be tailing Thursday, the master PENGUIN spy.

Bartholomew knew Eddy too. After all, it was Eddy's father who had made 'The Source' what he was. But Eddy had no idea who Bartholomew was. They'd actually met face-to-face just once. When Eddy was about 5 years old, after Eddy's dad disappeared, he'd seen Bartholomew in the back yard of his house. Eddy tried to catch the little green frog. But because of Bartholomew's talent, he wasn't quite up to the task. Before Eddy caught him, Bartholomew had disappeared. But Bartholomew didn't just disappear and never come back. No, Bartholomew kept coming back, just as he'd been doing since Eddy was a baby. Again and again and again Bartholomew

30

came back. Eddy didn't know it, but Bartholomew spent a lot of time in his room. Most every night, Bartholomew watched Eddy go to sleep. Often, he even stayed all night, making sure nothing happened to the kid. More than anything else, even sauteed flies and cola, Bartholomew loved to sit on the Gryffin's table and watch Eddy sleep.

Bartholomew wished he could hop to where Eddy's dad was and fix everything right then and there. But he couldn't – for some reason, that hop was beyond his powers. Instead he sat there and comforted himself by guarding his mentor's son through uneventful nights. He could never repay Eddy's dad, but he could protect his son.

And now, Short Eddy was following Thursday to a top secret meeting with Sam the Elephant. A meeting that involved a dangerous plot to take over the entire world.

Bartholomew didn't know what to do. He thought about calling off the meeting, just to be safe. But as Thursday knew, when the 'The Source' had a story to spill it was important that he spill it. Grobar had to be stopped.

For now, Bartholomew decided to do what he did best. Watch.

Standing by the riverfront, Thursday pulled an ice cream out of his trenchcoat. The PENGUIN spy hadn't meant to be early. After a few minutes of licking the ice cream, Thursday saw the tip of Sam's trunk break the surface of the water. Sam was sniffing around cautiously. Thursday waited. He knew the drill. Thursday knew Sam always started their meetings this way. What Thursday didn't know was at that moment, just before Sam's head rose out of the water, Bartholomew hopped into the elephant's ear.

As the massive animal came partway out of the water, Thursday wondered, 'How can he be so big, and so quiet?'

Sam looked up and whispered, "Hey, Thursday good buddy, how's it goin'?"

It wasn't really a question. It was just a friendly hello. But Thursday answered him anyways, "It's going fine, Sam. You enjoy the macadamias?"

"Oh yeah, Thursday, I sure did," the elephant replied. "Those are my favorite nuts. Sometimes I feel like I could eat a whole truckload of them."

The elephant wasn't exaggerating. Thursday had seen him once when he was depressed about something or other. And that's exactly what he did. He ate a whole truckload of nuts.

"Word is," Thursday said, "that 'The Source' has got a story to spill."

"Always business, Thursday, aren't ya? The word would be right, there is a story. And it's a big one."

Sam stopped talking for a moment, then looked around carefully. One giant ear perked up. It looked like he was listening for unusual sounds. What Thursday didn't know was that 'The Source' was whispering in Sam's ear.

Thursday always got a little impatient in situations like these. He wanted to know the story. He felt like saying, "So, spill it." But he didn't. With Sam you just took your time. He'd let it all out eventually.

"Before I tell you the lowdown," Sam said, "I've got to let you know that 'The Source' is a little unhappy with you."

'Unhappy?' Thursday thought, trying to look like a very innocent penguin. But he knew exactly what Sam was talking about. Thursday had tried following Sam once, across the river. He wanted to see where he met 'The Source.' He wanted to figure out who 'The Source' really was. Bartholomew hadn't been so keen on the idea.

"Thursday," Sam said, "'The Source' knows you've been following me and trying to track him down. He wanted me to tell you that he doesn't like that much. He said he'd really appreciate it if you didn't try it again."

Thursday couldn't understand. He asked himself, silently, 'I can hug the shadows like a too-small sweater on a fat man. How could 'The Source' know I was following Sam?' Clearly, Thursday had underestimated 'The Source.' He imagined he wasn't the first person to do so. "Sorry 'bout that Sam," Thursday said. "It's my profession."

One of Sam's ears perked up again. Bartholomew whispered to him, "Tell him that if it happens again, I'm not giving him any more information."

With a sigh, Sam announced, "I know you're sorry, Thursday. And I know it's just your job. But you know what?"

"What?" Thursday asked.

Sam continued, almost jovially, "'The Source' told me you'd say exactly that. And he told me to tell you that the story spigot would get stopped up if you tried that stunt again. Not my words, Thursday, but I think we both know what he means."

"Sorry Sam," Thursday said, seriously. "It won't happen again." Thursday meant it, a good spy always keeps his word.

"Promise accepted!" Sam exclaimed with a giant smile on his face. Just like that, Thursday realized, once again, how good it felt to be Sam's friend. "Here's the story," Sam continued. "there's a goat named Grobar. As always, his location is unknown. He's planning to take over the world. According to 'The Source,' he's got some sort of secret recipe for turning caffeinated drinks into mind-control potions. The word is that he plans to poison the world's tea, coffee or soda with this concoction and thus gain control over a significant proportion of the population. The rest of the population, as 'The Source' explained it, would be liquidated."

Thursday wanted to know what the recipe was. He started to ask, "What's the- "

But Sam cut him off, "I'm ahead of you buddy. The recipe, and a lot of other information about Grobar, is already waiting in your office at the water park."

"Really?" whispered Bartholomew. As far as he knew, he hadn't put any information in Thursday's office. Sam replied with a single grunt. Thursday didn't notice, but Bartholomew did. One grunt generally meant 'yes.' In this case, one grunt meant 'Yes, the information needs to be in the office, and pronto.' So, Bartholomew hopped home, grabbed the memory chip that Thursday needed, hopped to Thursday's office, left the disk in the middle of his desk and jumped back to Sam's ear. The whole process was done in about 3 seconds. Bartholomew was happy he'd discovered memory chips. When you're a few inches long, secretly moving a file cabinet to a covert office under a waterpark pool can be a *bit* unwieldy.

"In my office?" asked Thursday, just as Bartholomew returned. The office was supposed to be secret. For a second, Thursday thought about moving. But then he realized it wouldn't have done any good. However 'The Source' did what he did, he probably wouldn't need the yellow pages to find Thursday's next base of operations.

"Thursday," Sam continued, "he's not going to tell anybody about your office, he just wanted to let you know how good he is and how much you'd miss his services if you tried to follow me again."

Thursday understood. He wasn't happy, but he understood. He knew he couldn't take it out on Sam. Last time Thursday checked, Sam couldn't possibly have fit in his office.

"So that's it," Sam concluded. "I'll let you know if 'The Source' learns more."

"Thanks again," Thursday replied, back to being all business. "I'll send you some more nuts tomorrow."

"I'd like that," said Sam jovially, just before he silently slipped back into the water.

Thursday turned around and walked towards his car. Out of the corner of his eye, he saw Short Eddy crouching – binoculars to his eyes.

Thursday was pretty impressed that the kid had tracked him all the way to the riverfront. Thankfully, Eddy'd gotten there too late. The kid didn't know anything, and Thursday, for the kid's own sake, was determined to keep it that way. The two of them were going to have to have a little talk.

Without breaking his stride, Thursday hopped into his little sports car and sped towards his not-so-secret-anymore office.

Pushing Short Eddy and the invasion of his office out of his mind, Thursday concentrated on the important thing.

Somewhere out there, there was an evil goat who Thursday had to stop.

(SHORT EDDY)

Northwest

Okay, I'll admit it. I was pretty happy that I'd managed to find Thursday.

I biked a little closer to him, slowly and quietly. And then I slipped off the bike and tried to figure out what was going on. Thursday was standing on the riverfront wall. I could see that he was talking to someone in the river. I would have stuck my head over the side to see who it was, but that would have given me away. So I crouched down against the riverfront wall and waited. I'd figure out what Thursday was up to sooner or later. I was only there for about thirty seconds when the conversation ended. Thursday waved his little wing and then jumped off the wall.

I watched him get in his little car and speed away.

Now was my chance.

I rushed up to where he'd been. He'd been talking to someone and I was going to find out who it was. I peered over the wall and do you know what I saw? It took a while, but I saw something gray just beneath the surface of the water. It looked almost like the top of a whale.

And it was swimming across the river!

I hopped on my bike and took off. I started pedaling as fast as I could towards the nearest bridge. Whatever it was, it might come out on the other side of the river and if it did, I was going to be there waiting for it. I started biking across the bridge as quickly as I possibly could. I was makin' time!

Before coming back down the other side of the bridge though, I stopped my bike and trained my binoculars on the water. I quickly spotted the gray-backed thing. Whatever it was, it was still crossing the river. I drew a path with my binoculars and figured out exactly where it was going. It was headed straight towards a boat ramp.

I headed down the other side of the bridge.

The boat ramp is on the northwest side of the river. The penguin had been on the southeast side. Southeast is the commercial part of town. There are lots of office towers and clean looking parks. The other side of the river, northwest, is completely different. It is heavily industrial. It seems almost coated with dirt and grime. Most people consider Northwest pretty boring, but I think it's really exciting.

You see, Northwest is a part of town that most kids haven't seen. I mean, we occasionally go on school trips to visit a paper plant there, but most kids don't just happen to wander around there to see what's going on. I think they're missing something. Northwest is one of the most exciting parts of Lakedale. There is always something going on in Northwest. And I don't mean things like Mean Eyes Paine beating up some first grader. I mean really really interesting things. For example, no matter when you visit, there's always something going on in the shipyards. They are unloading and loading ships and trains all day and sometimes all night. You can also go see the factories. In one, they make truck engines. In another, they make soda bottles. One place out on the outskirts of Northwest even makes pharmaceuticals. Basically, there is always lots going on. If you like watching things get put together or taken apart or moved around, then Northwest is the place to be.

And Northwest was the place where the gray thing in the water was heading.

When I got to the other side of the bridge, I scanned the river with my binoculars. The gray thing was still on course. It was getting closer to the boat ramp. It seemed like forever, but eventually it got there. And then, it started to come out of the river. It sure wasn't a whale, but I didn't know what it was. When I watched it come out of the water I should have recognized it immediately, but I didn't. It just didn't connect. It took like 30 seconds before I actually believed what I was seeing. You see, the thing Thursday had been talking to, the gray thing that had been crossing the river – it was a huge elephant.

Yes, you heard me right. An elephant. Swimming across the river. Right there in downtown Lakedale.

I couldn't understand it. What was an elephant doing in the city? There weren't even any elephants in the zoo. I was really confused. But the elephant was right there, right in front of me, walking out of the water. I couldn't deny that it was there. As I watched the elephant, I realized that there was something really odd about it. I mean, something really odd *aside* from it being in the middle of the city. You see, the elephant was crouching low to the ground and looking this way and that. The elephant looked like it was trying to hide. But the elephant didn't have any of Thursday's smooth stealth. It seemed very nervous, like it didn't want anybody to see it, but it wasn't good enough at hiding to prevent being seen. I couldn't imagine something that big being good at hiding anyways.

The elephant shouldn't have worried too much. At that time of night, the Northwest side of the waterfront was pretty much empty. I mean, he couldn't have predicted that I'd be there. But otherwise, he didn't have to worry much. Only a few factories were open at this time of night, and everybody was working in them – not hanging around outside. There was nobody on the streets.

Nonetheless, there the elephant was, walking real close to the ground and looking something like a giant crab-walking Navy SEAL. The elephant crossed the riverfront park that way. When it got to the first building, it peeked around it and down the street it was on. There wasn't anybody on the street. So BAM! just like that the elephant took off down the street at a full gallop. I was biking as fast as I could to keep up, but elephants are faster than they look. I was afraid I was going to lose the big guy. I felt a little stupid. You know you aren't very good at following things when you can't keep track of an elephant in the middle of a city. It wasn't like it was some sort of anonymous taxicab. But then the elephant just stopped. It stopped just short of the next intersection. It gave me plenty of time to catch up while it stuck its head out into the street and looked both ways before crossing it. Then, once again, BAM! he took off across the street and all the way up to the next block. It was trying very very hard to make very very sure that nobody saw it. I don't know how it missed me. The elephant kept going like that for almost a mile, peeking around buildings and sprinting up blocks – before it finally got where it was going – a warehouse that was right next to a massive junkyard. There was a sign above the door. It read, "ACME TOE JAM AND TOAST." It was the kind of place few people would randomly visit.

I watched from a distance as the elephant used his trunk to pull a key out of a pouch attached to his leg. The elephant then used that key to open the warehouse door. The door slid open on its tracks revealing a blast of light from inside. I was impressed. I had never seen an elephant use a key before. Hey, I had never even seen an elephant before. From my angle, I couldn't see anything inside the warehouse. But I was outside the junkyard gates and the junkyard was right next to the warehouse. I didn't see any "DANGER: KILLER DOG WAITING TO TEAR YOU TO SHREDS" signs on the junkyard gate, so I crawled under it and into the yard. There were stacks of cars all over. They didn't look very stable and I didn't want to climb on them. I could see that the warehouse the elephant was in had high up windows. I really wanted to peek inside through them. There was a little roof that ran along right beneath them. I thought that if I could get up to that roof, I could look inside the building. I looked around for a bit before I finally saw it. This old utility vehicle was sitting right next to the wall. You know the kind of utility vehicle that the phone company uses to go up to the top of phone poles. They have that platform and a control button on the platform that lets them move up and down. I was pretty lucky that the vehicle was there, but there it was. I quickly climbed onto the platform and hit the "UP" button. In a few moments, I was level with the warehouse windows. Thankfully, the vehicle didn't make very much noise.

I scrambled up onto the warehouse roof and looked in the windows. The entire warehouse was one big open space. Along one wall there, was a giant bookcase. Along another wall, there was what was probably the world's largest mini-kitchen. The kitchen was dominated by a giant sink and enough counter space to stick a cow on. In the middle of the room, there was a huge bed with a really, really thick mattress. There was also a really big screen TV and a giant bag of marshmallows. It took me longer to figure out than it should have, but eventually, it dawned on me. This was where the elephant lived. I expected the elephant to go for the marshmallows, after all, they are known to be very hungry animals. But the elephant did nothing of the sort. He just headed straight towards bed. He took the pouch off his leg (the one that had his house keys) and then lay down and fell asleep.

I thought about going for the marshmallows myself.

Well, not really, although they were really really tempting.

The fact was, I was very happy with what I had accomplished and I didn't want to blow it. I knew where the elephant lived, so I could always come back later.

I went back down to the junkyard, crawled under the gate and then hopped back on my bike. I biked all the way home in one stretch. It took forever and I was very tired when I got home. I climbed back up the tree and into my room. As I was changing into my James Bond pajamas, I noticed that a piece of paper had been slipped under my door. I picked it up and turned on the light to read it. It read, "Meet me. 3pm, my place, Thursday."

I would've have run right over to the waterpark to talk to him. But he didn't want to meet tomorrow. Plus, it was getting really late and I was pretty tired. So, I went to the bathroom to brush my teeth and then I came back and went straight to bed.

Even though I was extremely tired, I had a hard time falling asleep. The note didn't help much. So much cool stuff had happened. In one day, I had learned about a secret office beneath the waterpark pool. I had met Thursday the penguin. I had tailed that same penguin to a secret meeting. And then I had followed the elephant the penguin had met there all the way back home to his junkyard. I replayed everything that had happened in my head. I could remember it all. But there was one huge hole. You see, I didn't know what Thursday and the elephant had talked about.

I wanted to know.

Perhaps Thursday would tell me when I went to meet him.

It had been a very exciting day.

(NARRATOR)

The Tip of the Iceberg

Have you ever seen one of those movies where they have a giant mission control room? Inside the room they have banks of computers and people working on all sorts of anonymous tasks? Sometimes the control room is for a NASA mission; sometimes it is for a military operation. You know how serious everybody always is in them – 'Rogers' and 'Yes, sirs' and 'No, sirs' flying around like Jello in a food fight? This control room was exactly like that – with one big difference. It wasn't filled with engineers or scientists or generals. Well, not normal engineers or scientists or generals. Instead, it was filled with almost 30, wing-flapping, waddling, birds – penguins to be exact.

The penguin control room is located almost one mile beneath the surface of the Antarctic ice shelf. Antarctica is the center of all penguin life. But penguin life is not quite what many think it is. Most people imagine penguins as wide waddling water-birds sunning themselves on some southern beach. But there's more going on. All the world's penguins – from every breed – belong to a secret organization called PENGUIN. PENGUIN stands for Penguins Engaged in Guarding a ... Well, the UIN part doesn't actually stand for anything. The fact that they couldn't make all the letters mean something wasn't enough to stop them from using it. It just seemed perfectly appropriate.

What is PENGUIN? PENGUIN is a secret organization engaged
in protecting the world from evil masterminds. PENGUIN has operatives all over the world. While the KGB (now known as the FSB),
CIA, MI-6 or the Mossad might not admit it, or even know it, PEN-
GUIN is the most important of all intelligence agencies.

So how come you haven't heard of it? Well, anonymity is the
secret behind all good intelligence agencies. The better they are, the
less people know about them. PENGUIN is so good that nobody has
ever heard of it. Even the other intelligence agencies are completely
in the dark. In order to hide its identity, PENGUIN is very careful
about a whole range of things – most importantly communications. If
someone were to intercept PENGUIN communications, then the
show would be over. So PENGUIN often uses alternative communications methods. Remember that image you had of wide waddling
water-birds sunning themselves on some southern beach? Well, those
penguins aren't just sunning themselves. They are actually posi-
tioning themselves and moving around in special patterns –
encrypted patterns that can be observed and interpreted by looking
at satellite videos of Antarctica. These patterns are the backbone of
PENGUIN's outgoing communications. Each PENGUIN field agent,
whether in America or Azerbaijan, has a device that downloads and
interprets the messages coming from Antarctica. It is all automatic.
The devices even have an extra feature. Unless a unique activation
code is entered, the devices look and behave like portable game
machines – nothing more. You can even play Tetris on them.

The whole waddling PENGUIN thing is used to send messags
from headquarters. But how do PENGUIN agents send messages *to*
headquarters? The answer is simple. While lots of people would
notice radio signals coming from Antarctica, nobody would notice
radio waves going *to* Antarctica. There are lots of those already –
although they aren't generally intended for *recipients* in Antarctica.
PENGUIN field agents can communicate with their home base by

sending encrypted static over a short-wave radio. Anybody can listen to the static, but PENGUIN HQ can actually decrypt the messages. It's all a very advanced system that completely hides the identity and existence of the world's top intelligence agency.

The biggest challenge for the Antarctic penguins is coordinating with the field agents – not communicating with them. Because Antarctica is on the bottom of the world, it doesn't have night and day quite like most places. So, there really aren't any times zones there. Humans have time zones they use in Antarctica, but they are pretty much made up. In order to address the time zone problem, PENGUIN HQ actually shifts time zones to whatever time zone has the most current activity. By default, when not much is going on, they are on Hawaiian time. Hard working PENGUIN agents have been known to hang out on beaches that are warmer than those back home.

Of course, they couldn't be on Hawaiian time all the time.

That evening, at exactly 7:23pm Hawaiian time, an unusual transmission came in. Two things happened. One, the communications men instructed the penguins on the surface to send back a response. Two, the time zone immediately changed. With a single transmission it became late night.

The control room was normally a pretty exciting place. It was almost always filled with a bunch of birds busily moving around with headsets on and sitting on chairs that are too tall for them (every chair was big enough for the largest bird in the room). But everybody there knew that it was about to get a whole lot more exciting.

A message had come in.

It wasn't just any message though.

It had been sent by a top-notch North American agent – Agent Thursday. He didn't send many messages, but when he did, it was to say something important. There was something else that made the message even more important. While Thursday had sent it, it had really come from none other than 'The Source.'

Because of that, the machinery of the world's greatest intelligence agency was about to get churning.

As Short Eddy lay in bed trying to fall asleep, the bottom of the world was about to get turned upside down.

(NARRATOR)

Ant House

Remember back when Bartholomew overheard Grobar shouting, "Ah ha, I've got it!" and then proceeding to dictate his entire plan to his computer? You might imagine that this genius of a goat had a tremendous mental breakthrough. But you'd be mistaken. The pieces for his plan had been staring him in the face for months already. All he did that day was put them together.

For years before Grobar knew he needed to take over the world, he had been spending his time wandering the plains of his native land. While wandering, he'd noticed an anthill somewhere in the oceans of grass. Most people wouldn't have cared about, or even noticed, this anthill, but Grobar noticed that sort of thing.

Ants have a quality that utopian-minded philosophers everywhere are always talking about. Ants seem to work in perfect harmony. It is almost like they have a single brain that carries out all their decision-making. It makes for fascinating watching. A lot of people, from biologists to communists, are very interested in how, exactly, ants pull this off. But nobody has been able to find out. The reason for this is simple: nobody has ever bothered to actually ask the ants themselves.

Grobar wasn't very good at connecting the dots, but he was superb at finding those dots. He paid careful attention to everything

46

that was going on around him. He noticed everything his human mother did. He noticed everything the people and things around him did. He also noticed how all the ants seemed to cooperate so perfectly. Being a curious fellow, he walked up to the anthill and said, "Excuse me, anybody home?" Grobar was raised to be polite. He would have knocked, but he was afraid of crushing something.

The queen ant, sensing that she was being called for, popped her head above the anthill. She was somewhat annoyed at the interruption to her daily chores. "Yes, what is it?" she asked.

"Uh, sorry to bother you, Mrs. Ant," said Grobar, "I was just curious, how do you keep all the little ants working together so nicely?"

"Oh, that," said the queen ant, "We queen ants use a recipe handed down from mother to daughter for generations. It is thousands of years old, at least."

Grobar was still curious. He asked, "Can I have a copy?"

The queen ant looked him up and down and he *looked* like a friendly goat. He seemed a little sad, but nobody could be blamed for being unhappy. She thought for a moment and then said, "Okay." With that, she closed her eyes.

Moments later, an army of stick-bearing ants came streaming out of the hill. Like a precision marching band they took up positions in the grass.

Grobar watched as they spelled out the first ingredient with their sticks:

"5 Washington State Apples."

The ants marched around some more and then the sticks wrote:

"4 New Zealand Kiwis."

And again the ants goose-stepped and then the sticks wrote:

"2 Gallons of Somali Camel's Milk,"

The sticks kept moving around as they spelled out the rest of the recipe:

"A tiny bit of water."

"Mix up, bake and then crush."

"Finally, package with caffeine."

"And deliver in liquid form."

Grobar was very impressed, and a bit confused. "Why," he asked, "didn't you just tell me the recipe?"

The Queen Ant said, warmly, "Sometimes we queen ants just like doing things the old fashioned way."

"I understand," said Grobar. He thought for a bit and then asked, "But, Mrs. Queen Ant, how do you, living here in the middle of nowhere, get all these ingredients?"

The Queen Ant answered, a smile on her tiny face, "Through the International Confederation of Queen Ants of course! We use the Flying Ant Service to move them around."

"Oh," said Grobar, "I guess that makes sense."

Grobar memorized the recipe. Then he said, "Thank you, Mrs. Queen Ant."

"You're welcome," came the reply from the tiny bug.

Grobar hesitated for a minute. The Queen Ant looked at him curiously. Getting his courage up, he asked, "Uh, Mrs. Queen Ant," he paused again, and then said, "uh, do you think I could move in with you?"

The Queen Ant smiled and said, "I'm sorry, but we just don't have the space."

Grobar smiled, weakly, and said, "Well, thanks anyway."

Then, he just meandered away.

The Queen Ant watched him go.

He seemed like such a friendly goat.

A Drug That Works

When Bartholomew discovered that Eddy had been watching
Thursday on the riverfront, he decided that the kid had earned at
least something for his troubles. He wasn't going to tell him about
Grobar the Goat; that would have put him in too much danger. But
he was going to let him get a brand new friend. The kid didn't have
many friends and Bartholomew – the nice frog that he was – had one
very big one to spare. Eddy's father's son deserved at least that
much.

When Eddy started following Sam home, Bartholomew was
ready. He told Sam to do his normal act – hiding behind buildings
and the such. But he also told Sam to completely ignore the kid
chasing him on a little bicycle. Bartholomew had decided that he
wanted Eddy to find Sam's home. He wanted Eddy to figure out what
it was, and he wanted him to come back later. Bartholomew didn't
move the utility truck to the side of Sam's warehouse, that was just a
coincidence – but it worked out well. After an evening of hard work,
Eddy had found Sam. And Bartholomew knew the two of them would
become best friends.

Bartholomew's night didn't end there though. When Thursday
transmitted his message to Antarctica, Bartholomew was ready. He
made one quick hop to PENGUIN HQ, cola in hand. Nobody noticed

49

the green frog holding the red can in the white room full of two-color Penguins. Bartholomew knew they wouldn't. He'd done it many times before. When Thursday's message came in, Bartholomew was drinking his soda. Waiting. He watched as the PENGUIN organization swung into motion. He was there to see if they needed help – and to provide it when they did.

It only took a few minutes for PENGUIN HQ to confirm Agent Thursday's message. The penguin pattern communications system was not the fastest in the world. However, after an exchange of secret codes, Agent Thursday's identity – and the validity of his message – were confirmed. Agent Thursday had sent the complete details of a plan to take over the world. It was an intricate and involved plan: Grobar the Goat – the evil mastermind – planned to poison caffeinated drinks with a special mind control potion. Using his newfound potion, he planned to take over the world.

PENGUIN HQ now knew the task that faced them. They had to find Grobar's location. You see, Agent Thursday had sent out a complete dossier that identified almost all aspects of the plot – including the drug ingredients – but one critical piece was missing. The dossier didn't say *where* either Grobar or his facilities were. It was a continuing mystery to the birds at PENGUIN HQ; for reasons they couldn't work out, 'The Source' almost never revealed the location of the evil mastermind. Unlike you, the Reader, the birds at PENGUIN HQ didn't know about Bartholomew and the limitations of his Precision Hopping Ability. They had no idea where or how 'The Source' got his information. They only knew that he almost never said where the bad guy was. More than a few penguins speculated that 'The Source' did it just to give PENGUIN a sense of accomplishment.

Chief Shift Officer July read Agent Thursday's message carefully. CSO July (yes, CSO means Chief Shift Officer) was an Empire Penguin – one of the big guys you see on Antarctic beaches. Only in this case, July was one of the big gals.

50

July was an unusual officer in that she hadn't always been on the PENGUIN intelligence team. Most high-ranking officers were career spy penguins. July wasn't. She had actually spent many years as a member of the PENGUIN Marine Corps. She was a specialist in beach raids, although she was certainly knowledgeable about other military maneuvers. Due to her many years in the Marines, July was a very strong penguin – both physically and personally. Although she was always friendly, the other penguins had a great deal of respect for her. When she spoke, everybody listened. She was just that kind of bird.

Thursday's message was projected on a giant screen at the front of the room. Officially it was up there for CSO July to read, but every penguin in that room was watching it carefully. Every penguin but one, that is. Officer Fortnight, the Chief Communications Officer, was watching CSO July. Fortnight had already read the message three times. She already knew what it said. Fortnight was a very fast penguin. She typed quickly. She thought quickly. Everything about her conveyed speed and efficiency. She was a little gal. She spoke quickly. Her eyes were constantly moving around. She also was a well-tailored penguin, who wore suit pants and a professional blouse and tie. They fit her perfectly. She was an ideal Communications officer – curt, to the point, and extremely efficient. She was looking at CSO July because she needed to know what CSO July wanted done.

July said, "First things first. Inform the Commander-in-Chief about the situation."

Fortnight typed a few quick sentences. The penguins on the ice-covered surface of Antarctica moved in their specially encoded patterns. The Commander-in-Chief, a human who didn't live in Antarctica, had the message by the time Fortnight turned back to July. The Commander-in-Chief responded immediately. The message was short and to the point, "Make this the only priority."

July read through the recipe again. She thought for a bit, her wing on her chin. Then she said, "Four ingredients, that's it? It seems a little easy."

Fortnight spoke up, "Well, sir, five actually. Caffeine needs to be there as the catalyst." Everybody referred to July as 'sir.' She didn't like 'madam.' It just seemed too wussy.

"Ah yes," said July, "Five. Washington State Apples, New Zealand Kiwi Fruit, Somalian Camel's Milk, a bit of heavy water and caffeine of any sort. An unusual mix. Do you think it will work?"

If you have been paying careful attention, you might have noticed that heavy water wasn't in the Queen Ant's recipe. This isn't a typo.

The biological weapons specialist, Expert Aries, who had a Ph.D. from P.I.T. (the Penguin Institute of Technology), answered, "It just might, sir. To my knowledge, nobody has ever combined those five ingredients. I don't quite see how it would work, and it does seem a little far fetched. However, I'm not prepared to write it off."

Carefully considering her words, July responded, "Is there any way you could answer that question more definitively?"

Aries had an annoying habit of chewing on the end of his right wing. While July talked to him, he was doing exactly that. It drove some of the other penguins mad, but Aries was such an excellent member of the PENGUIN team that nobody even mentioned his nervous habit to him. They figured he must have noticed it. After all, a chewed wing meant a slower commute to PENGUIN HQ. After about 5 additional seconds of wing chewing Aries spoke, "Yes, sir. Absolutely. We could make a batch ourselves and try it out. The risk is that we might do irreparable damage to our tester's brain."

"Any other ideas?" asked July. She wasn't delighted with that solution.

"Yes, sir!" shouted Trainee Midday, a young energetic penguin who was in the HQ for the first time in his short career. He was a Chinstrap penguin.

"Well, spit it out, Midday."

"Yes, sir!" shouted Trainee Midday. He thought for a bit, unused to actually speaking in the HQ. This was the first time he had ever said anything. "Well sir, the goat must have tried it out on somebody. He must know whether or not it works. What we have to do is find someone who has been drugged."

"Midday," said CSO July, "rhat is a superb idea. Does anybody know how we might find such a person?"

"Let's ask 'The Source'!" piped up Trainee Midday. He'd forgotten his 'Yes, sirs!' and 'No, sirs!' in the excitement.

July thought it was a great idea. So did 'The Source.'

Unbeknownst to the penguins, Bartholomew was already on his way.

In a super-hop (that's what he liked to call them), Bartholomew was gone. Nobody saw him disappear. It helped that nobody saw him in the first place. He made a quick stop by his house to recycle his cola can and then he made one more super-hop. To the location of a person who had been drugged by Grobar.

At the end of that super-hop, he found himself in the office of an obviously wealthy man. The man was facing away from Bartholomew. He was looking out the windows behind his desk. He was looking away from Bartholomew. Of course, Bartholomew had expected this. He never super-hopped into the line of sight of his targets. A quick glance out the window, and Bartholomew recognized that he was in Atlanta. Not wanting to stick out, Bartholomew hopped to the man's bookshelf. It was covered with kitsch and provided the perfect camouflage. Bartholomew did an excellent job of looking like a highly realistic porcelain frog.

Bartholomew didn't know who the man was, but he could certainly make an educated guess.

53

When the man turned around, Bartholomew's guess – and his greatest fears – were confirmed. The man was none other than William McGrover, Chief Executive Officer of SodaCo. McGrover didn't notice Bartholomew. He just sat at his desk, working. He had a slightly glazed look about him. He didn't look like he was all there. The problem was, Bartholomew didn't know enough about him to blame Grobar's drug for his condition. He might just be the glazed type. Bartholomew would have to observe him more to determine whether Grobar's drug was at fault.

After about a minute, the man gathered up some papers and headed out the door. Bartholomew could have followed him by conventionally hopping. However, Bartholomew always felt exposed normal-hopping around enemy territory like an ordinary frog. People knew what frogs did. If Bartholomew's actions matched his appearance, his chances of being noticed would rise exponentially. When he was observing someone, Bartholomew almost never moved in the conventional way. This time was no exception. Instead of normal-hopping after McGrover, he super-hopped to wherever it was McGrover was going.

It turned out to be SodaCo's boardroom.

It was a beautiful boardroom. Bartholomew immediately liked it. He quickly reminded himself to come back and visit some other time. The room had wall-to-wall burled walnut and an expansive view of the city of Atlanta. In preparation for a meeting, there were delicate pastries, bountiful fruit and of course Bartholomew's favorite cola – all supplied in quantity. Bartholomew briefly considered grabbing a snack, but he was here on business. If he sat still, nobody would see him. But if he were slurping a soda, he'd definitely get noticed. The boardroom slowly filled with executives. Most of them grabbed a pastry or fruit – and a soda. Not one noticed Bartholomew.

Then Chief Executive McGrover strode in – still wearing that glazed look. McGrover was an extremely smooth man. His jaw was so sharp it looked like it had been cut from glass. His closely cropped hair conveyed a no-nonsense approach to business. He had a widespread reputation as a master orator and a very emotional speaker. McGrover strode to the front of the boardroom then turned around to face SodaCo's board of directors. And then he started talking. But, his voice wasn't emotional. It was almost robotic. Even with his limited knowledge, Bartholomew could tell this probably wasn't the normal McGrover.

"Ladies and Gentlemen," said McGrover, "I have called this meeting to discuss adding a second secret ingredient to our famed line of cola drinks. For the past thirty years, our market share has remained roughly stagnant. We have been locked in a neck-to-neck battle with GoodDrinks, Inc. CEO after CEO has tried to find a way to win the battle without getting into a profit slashing price war. All have failed. And so, while we are hugely profitable, we find ourselves in an uncomfortable battle with GoodDrinks. We need to address the problem. A second secret ingredient is the key to increasing our market share."

All around the boardroom, jaws dropped. Bartholomew knew what he had to know. The drug worked. As a dedicated drinker of SodaCo Cola, Bartholomew knew that you just didn't mess with the secret recipe. While Bartholomew wanted to stick around and see what would transpire, his work was done. He really had wanted to know whether he could continue to enjoy the thirst-quenching refreshing taste of his favorite cola. But other tasks called him. He had to get PENGUIN the news that the drug worked. For now, he would just have avoid drinking the stuff.

Just before he super-hopped away, Chief Executive McGrover said, in the same robotic voice, "What is that frog doing in this boardroom."

Before McGrover had even finished his sentence, Bartholomew was gone.

The board members all looked where McGrover was pointing. But none of them saw a frog. And none of them saw anyplace a frog could possibly hide. In the wood, steel and glass of the boardroom, something like a frog would certainly have stuck out. Finally, the chairman of the board, whose great-grandfather had founded SodaCo, turned to McGrover. He whispered with authority, "That does it, you've really lost your marbles."

In a vote of 14-1, the 1 being McGrover himself, Chief Executive Officer William McGrover of SodaCo was fired. Company security escorted him, shouting and struggling, out of the boardroom and out of the building. Only then did Grobar release him from the mind control, leaving him on the sidewalk, with no memory of what had occurred.

Thanks to Bartholomew's coincidental timing, Grobar's first attempt to access the caffeinated beverage market had failed completely.

SodaCo soda, and the world, were safe.

For the time being.

(NARRATOR)

PENGUIN and the Potion

July sent an encrypted message to Agent Thursday, asking him to see if the 'The Source' could check whether the drug worked. And then her team in the HQ got back to work.

"So," said July, "assuming that the drug does work – which we have to assume until we learn otherwise – what can we do to find Grobar or the factory he's gonna use to make the drug?"

Grobar's version of the queen ant's recipe was shining on the overhead monitor.

Grobar's Mind Control Potion Recipe
Mix:

      500 minced Washington State Apples

      400 minced New Zealand Kiwis

      200 Gallons of Somali Camel's Milk

      5 Gallons of Heavy Water

Cook at 400F for 30 minutes.

Freeze dry.

Crush into a fine powder using sonic waves.

Mix with caffeinated drink.

Controls 100,000 people.
Serve chilled or hot.

Nobody knew how to find Grobar or the factory – but everybody was thinking extremely hard. And then, once again, Trainee Midday spoke up, "I have an idea, sir!"

"Yes?" asked July.

"Well sir, if he wants to poison the entire developed world, he will need a lot of the above ingredients. Perhaps, sir, we can track major purchases?"

July was impressed. "Midday, we will have to talk in my office after this is over. That is another excellent suggestion. First, put up the total amounts of each ingredient that Grobar will need."

After a moment, the screen changed. Each of the quantities had been multiplied by 10,000.

Grobar's Mind Control Potion Recipe
Mix:

    5 million Washington State Apples
    4 million New Zealand Kiwi
    2 million gallons of Somali Camel's Milk
    50,000 gallons of Heavy Water

Cook at 400F for 30 minutes.
Freeze dry.
Crush into a fine powder using sonic waves.
Mix with caffeinated drink.

Controls One Billion people.
Serve chilled or hot.

July asked the agricultural specialist, Expert Pisces, "Pisces, do you know how much of these products are produced each year?"

Pisces was a medium-sized penguin of the Adelie breed who wore burlap trousers and a thick set of suspenders. He looked like an old-time farmer. All that he was missing was a corn cob pipe. He also talked like a farmer. He had a real country accent. Expert Pisces might have looked like a backwoods character. But he had an uncanny understanding of all things agricultural. He also knew how to use a computer. Pisces responded, "Well boss, I can give you an answer on the apples, kiwi and camel's milk. I'm afraid the heavy water is outside my domain. Perhaps Expert Leo would know that. Give me a bit 'a time to work the other stuff out."

Expert Leo was PENGUIN's nuclear specialist.

Why would a nuclear specialist know about heavy water?

Here's a little history. Heavy water is important for nuclear reactors and atom bombs. The Nazis, the Russians and the Americans all made it during World War II. A group of 9 Norwegian commandos saved the world by destroying Hitler's heavy water production facility in a daring raid in which no shots were fired. Unbeknownst to most people, including the Norwegians, they were secretly assisted by PENGUIN agents.

In a physical sense, heavy water is very similar to regular water except, as you might have guessed, it is heavier. This is because the hydrogen atoms in H_2O (water) have been replaced with deuterium atoms. Deuterium is identical to hydrogen except that it has an extra neutron. It all sounds pretty complex. It is. If you want to learn more and your dad or mom is a physicist – go ask them. If they aren't physicists, read another book or go to nuclear engineering school. This book is about a secret agent penguin, a 10 year-old kid and an evil goat. You can't really expect an in-depth explanation of heavy water, can you?

Expert Leo, like your mom or dad if they are nuclear specialists, knew a lot about heavy water. Unlike your mom or dad, he was a Rockhopper penguin (well, your parents might be Rockhopper penguins, but we'll assume they aren't). Even if your parents are nuclear specialists, Expert Leo may have known more about heavy water than they do. This is because he concerned himself with everything nuclear – not just the physics, but also the politics, economics and statistics of nuclear stuff. Expert Leo didn't just know more about heavy water than most nuclear physicist parents – he also looked nothing like them. Expert Leo was short, wore a kilt and liked to talk in a Scottish accent, even though there aren't any native Scottish penguins. It was all a pretty good ploy. Except for the very nerdy and large glasses constantly perched on his beak. That, and the fact that his Scottish accent was very bad.

"Sir," said Expert Leo, "da fiyve contr's dat provide figus maak a'boot tirty-fiyve undred toons of 'eavy wata. No' a wee bit o da stuff. Accordin-"

July interrupted him, "Drop the accent Leo."

"Sorry, sir," said Leo, speaking normally. He didn't like speaking normally. "According to our numbers, the countries that don't give numbers make another six thousand tons of heavy water per year. However, this supply is heavily guarded. Technically, the five countries that create heavy water don't actually create it; it is already in regular water, it just has to be separated out."

"Thank you, Leo," said July. She sometimes wished Leo didn't add extra bits of irrelevant information. For some reason, all nerdy guys like him liked to show off their knowledge. July knew that accepting quirks like that was part of the price you paid to have their immense brains around. "How much of the world supply is 50,000 gallons?" she asked.

Expert Leo responded instantly, "Heavy water weighs almost ten pounds per gallon. Well, it is actually closer to 9.996 pounds per gallon. So if he needs 50,000 gallons he needs about 500,000 pounds of heavy water. As I gave the world supply in tons, I should convert it. As each ton is 2000 pounds, he actually needs about 250 tons of the stuff. He's looking at a fair chunk of the 3500 possibly available tons produced, or about 7%. Did you know that 7% of the world's geese are scared of spiders?"

"Thank you," said July, ignoring the last bit of information. "Is there any other way he can get the heavy water he needs?"

"Well," said Leo, "He could make it himself. He would need some real experts though. Making heavy water is a very tricky process. It also costs more than buying it. Heavy water costs about $100 per gallon. So he needs $5 million of the stuff. Making a heavy water plant will cost at least $10 million. Chances are very high that he will be buying the stuff – or already has. Also, we have to take into account that there are about 50,000 tons of stockpiled heavy water. He might be able to steal a very small part of that and thus meet his needs. Did you know goats like Grobar like clover?"

In fact, July knew that goats didn't like clover – at least not for long. Clover, if it wasn't mixed with something else, was poisonous to goats. But July didn't argue. Sometimes, it was hard to convince penguins like Leo to stay within their own fields of expertise. "So," said July, trying to stay on topic, "We need to try to cover all the bases. Assignments Officer Week, send field agents out to the heavy water plants or their controlling agencies to see if there have been any major purchases recently or if some of the supply has gone missing. We might be able to locate Grobar by working out a pattern in the purchases and or thefts of heavy water."

"Yes, sir!" said Assignments Officer Week, glad to finally be of use.

The agricultural specialist, Expert Pisces, spoke up, "While you've been working on heavy water, I've been looking into the other ingredients. The yearly production of Washington State Apples is 5 billion pounds. The yearly production of New Zealand Kiwis is 2 billion pounds. Grobar needs about 3 hundredths of a percent of the yearly supply of Washington State Apples and one tenth of a percent of the yearly supply of New Zealand Kiwis. It is highly unlikely that we'd be able to find Grobar's purchases considering the size of the market. But camel's milk is an entirely different story. There are 301 million gallons of Somali camel's milk produced a year. Grobar needs only 2 million gallons. This might normally be hard to detect, but – and you won't find this in any computer – camel's milk is very rarely exported. If Grobar is making his recipe somewhere outside of Somalia, then we'd be able to detect the camel's milk exports."

"Excellent," said July. "Officer Week, get our Somali agent on the case."

Week turned around and set himself to his task. Working with Fortnight, the two had the penguins on the surface moving in about 30 seconds. Almost immediately, the PENGUIN field agent in Somalia (where the camel's milk was from) and those in five other countries (that produced heavy water) got their assignments. Unfortunately, even those who were playing Tetris on their decoders were interrupted with their new orders. That's when they knew that the assignment was top priority.

"Well," said July, "that's about all we can do for now. It is very late so everybody get a good night's sleep. The backup crew will monitor things until tomorrow. Perhaps we'll have some information from 'The Source' by then."

It wasn't actually that late. The Penguins hadn't been awake for a full day. But because the time zone shifted when Thursday sent his message, it had suddenly become much later than it had been before. When the backup crew came in, July explained what had transpired to her replacement, Agent January. Then July's crew filed out of the room and January's crew filed in.

Despite the excitement of their work, the PENGUIN agents had no problem going straight to bed. They were completely professional and they all knew the importance of a good night's sleep.

Their hunt for Grobar would continue in the morning.

(SHORT EDDY)

A Bright Spring Day

Just seconds before I was actually conscious, I heard my mom's shrill, and totally familiar, "EDDY! IT'S TIME TO GET UP!" My brain had managed to put my mom's shout in the middle of one of my dreams. It was actually more of a nightmare. You see, I was lying down in some weird place, stuck to the floor, when Thursday the penguin started shouting at me, with my mother's voice, "EDDY! IT'S TIME TO GET UP!" He seemed really worried. I didn't know what was wrong, but it scared me. Of course, it turned out that the entire thing was just a dream. It was just my mom telling me to get out of bed like she did every morning.

As soon as I actually opened my eyes, I could see that it was a beautiful day. The sun was shining; the birds were chirping. I got up from my bed and I could see that even the grass seemed to be getting in on the good vibes – it was really green.

I got up, took a shower, got dressed and rushed downstairs. My mom was waiting.

"Hi, Mom!" I said.

"Glad to see you're awake, Eddy," she said, sarcastically. "Why are you so chipper?"

"I kinda of met this cool elephant last night. He was having a secret meeting with the penguin I told you about yesterday."

64

My mom's face just dropped, "Oh," she said, as she took out her little notebook.

"Yeah! So I'm going to go to his place today and see if I can get to talk to him."

"Well," said my mother, trying to put a good face on things, "It sounds like you have a busy day planned. You better eat breakfast first."

"Do I have to?" I asked.

"Yes," said my mom, "I'm sure the elephant you met has to eat breakfast too. Plus, I've already made French toast, your favorite."

"Okay," I said, as I reluctantly sat down at the table. My mom finished making her notes. She smiled a worried smile and then got me some piping hot French toast. It was drenched in syrup and it was actually really, really good. The thing was, even though it was my favorite food, I wasn't paying much attention. The only thing I could think about was hopping on my bicycle and heading towards the warehouse I'd seen the night before.

As soon as breakfast was done, I started to do exactly what I had been thinking about. I said, "Thanks, Mom," and rushed towards the door.

But my mom stopped me. "Eddy," she said, "I don't care what kind of animal you're meeting, you have to brush your teeth first."

I dashed upstairs, brushed my teeth, ran back downstairs, shouted, "Bye, Mom!" hopped on my bicycle and started peddling away. Even though I was peddling really fast, it seemed like it took forever to get to the elephant's warehouse.

I'll admit that I was a little worried that it had all been some strange dream and that neither the elephant nor the penguin were real. But I kept going. I got lots of strange looks from people on their way to work – I don't think they were used to a kid riding through downtown on a bicycle in the middle of rush hour.

When I finally got to the elephant's pad, I didn't know what to say. I mean, I had thought about it during the entire bike ride, but I didn't know how to introduce myself. What would you say to an elephant who lived in a warehouse who didn't know you from a banana tree? The best I could think of was, "Uh, hi, Mr. Elephant, my name's Eddy. I followed you home last night. Want to tell me about your clandestine conversation with the penguin?" As you can imagine, that wouldn't work very well.

Facing the elephant's front door, all I knew was that I had to knock on the door and get it over with. So I did. I knocked on the door, a big warehouse door. And guess what? Nobody answered. I thought maybe the whole thing had been a dream. I tried knocking again, harder. Again, nobody answered. Maybe the elephant wasn't home. Maybe he didn't even exist.

But I had biked all the way to the warehouse, so I wasn't about to give up yet. So I went next door, to the junkyard, and climbed up on the roof to see if I could spot the elephant inside. I crawled under the gate just as I had the night before. And, just like the night before, I headed straight towards the utility truck. It was right where I had remembered it being. And do you know what I saw out of the corner of my eye? Hidden behind a stack of cars was the elephant. I could see his gray skin through cracks in the pile. I had found him!

I shouted, "Hello, Mr. Elephant."

He didn't respond.

So I said, "I can see you, Mr. Elephant. You aren't hiding very well."

He still didn't respond.

So I walked over to the cars, intending to go around the back of them and confronting the elephant face to face. And do you know what the elephant did? It was like he was hiding behind a tree. When I walked to his side of the cars, he just walked around the stack to the other side of the cars. The stack of cars was still between him and me. He was still pretending that I hadn't seen him. So I walked around the stack to follow him. Once again, he circled around, keeping the cars between himself and me. I started running, and so did he. We were racing around the stack of cars, and I couldn't catch up. And then, all of a sudden, I just stopped and turned around. As I expected, the elephant came racing around the cars and almost ran into me. Luckily, he skidded to a stop in front of me, kicking dust up everywhere. If he had actually hit me, I would have been a Very Short Eddy pancake. He looked down at me, and I looked up at him. And then he said, in an incredibly deep voice that was almost like a whisper, "What do you want?"

And finally I knew what I wanted to say, "I heard an elephant lived here and I wanted to meet him."

He looked at me suspiciously. I got the idea that he didn't like strangers. Then he said, "Did you come here to stare at me?"

And I said, "Nope, I didn't come to stare. I came here because I've always wanted to meet an elephant. I heard they were very smart and very nice."

He looked at me, eyeing me carefully. "I don't like people who come to stare at me. I like my privacy."

I asked, "Why don't you like people to stare at you?"

The elephant leaned down to me and said, "I've never liked people staring at me. But I'm so big and I stick out so much that I can't avoid it. Whenever I go out for peanuts, everybody stares at me. I try to go out only at night, but even then people occasionally see me. And they point and stare at me and I just don't like it."

"Well, Mr. Elephant," I said, "I personally would like to be the center of attention. If I were like you, I would be kinda like a celebrity."

"Well I don't like being the center of attention," He said. His answer seemed very firm.

I liked attention, but I could still understand the elephant's problem. After all, it couldn't be much fun to *always* be the focus of attention. But I didn't have anything to say to him. It seemed like the conversation had reached a dead end. I stood there facing him, and he stood there facing me. And then, after what seemed like 5 minutes, the standoff finally ended.

"I like to go to parks," he said. "They can be lots of fun. Unfortunately I never go during the daytime because people see me."

It was a weird thing for him to say. But I guess he was trying to start a real conversation.

And then, just like that, I had an idea, "Mr. Elephant, I can take you to the park if you'd like. If I put you on a leash then everybody will think you're my pet elephant. They might look at you, but they'll look at me a lot more!"

The elephant seemed genuinely excited. His giant ears perked up and he whispered, again in that incredibly deep voice, "Do you think that would actually work?"

"Yup!" I pronounced, although I wasn't entirely sure that it would. "In fact, if you can find some string that's long enough we can go right now!"

He looked at me for a little bit. Weighing his options. But I could see I had him hooked. "Okay," he said. "I have string next door. I'll go get it and you stay here and then we'll go to the park."

And before I could even say "Okay" the big guy dashed off. He came back, almost panting, about a minute later. He had the string. He handed it me.

I took it. It was a pretty long piece of string. It would do.

I tried to throw it around the elephant's neck, but I was just too short. I couldn't reach over his neck. So the elephant got down on his knees and I climbed up on top of him and threw the string over. Then, I hopped off of him. When he stood up again, I moved underneath him, grabbed the string and tied it to itself. Just like that, I had an elephant leash. It was pretty cool. I mean, I never had a dog or anything, I'd never walked any animal on a leash, but now I had an elephant on a leash. Sure, he wasn't MY elephant, but he was still an elephant. It was pretty neat.

With the leash completed, the elephant and I headed out of the junkyard. Just before he closed and locked the gate he turned to me and said, "By the way, my name's Sam. What's yours?"

"Eddy," I responded. "Although lots of people call me Short Eddy."

He nodded and with that we started walking straight towards my neighborhood, where all the good parks are.

I hadn't even noticed that I'd left my bike behind.

(NARRATOR)

Demain

Somalia is hot. Very hot. It is all desert. While there is an ocean, it's the kind of ocean you only notice when you're in it. Otherwise all you notice is the sand, the desert and the heat. For a penguin it is one of the world's least comfortable assignments.

For an ambitious PENGUIN agent, it is also one of the world's greatest opportunities.

While Somalia is hot – which Penguins hate – it is also a source of international intrigue. All sorts of internationally intriguing people live in Somalia. There are slave traders, drug runners, terrorists and everything in between. In Somalia, there is a world of spying to be done. And very few penguins want to do it.

That was how Demain (French for Tomorrow), ended up there. He was an ambitious young PENGUIN agent. Like Agent Fortnight he was very efficient and curt. He also spoke with awesome clarity. Those who heard him felt like he was lifting a cloud of uncertainty from around their heads. Those who worked with him believed in him. Some of his commanders were so impressed with him that they thought he might eventually become a Chief Shift Officer. Secretly, he was aiming for a higher office – the office of the Commander-in-Chief.

70

While submitting his application for his first assignment as a full-fledged field agent, Demain had noticed Somalia standing vacant on the map. There were no PENGUIN agents there. Demain knew it was an important place and so he asked Personnel Officer April to station him there. April was a very careful officer. She asked him if he knew about the weather.

"Yes, I do," said Demain.

"And you're sure you want to go?" asked April.

With the confidence that he was famous for, Demain responded, "Yes, ma'am. I am sure."

And that was that. Demain was sent to Somalia. Specifically, he was sent to Mogadishu, the capital of Somalia.

Three months later, as he watched the hustle and bustle of the Mogadishu bazaar, he got his first assignment. His receiver read:

START URGENT TRANSMISSION
LOCATE CAMEL'S MILK EXPORTERS
IDENTIFY OVERSEAS BUYERS
CONVEY DATA TO HQ
END TRANSMISSION

Demain smiled when he got that assignment. It was exactly what he wanted. URGENT meant important.

Camel's milk is a very interesting commodity. Few people drink it. According to most reports, it just isn't very good. According to all reports, it is extremely strong. It is drunk slowly and with a great deal of reluctance. According to Bedouin legend, a child weaned on camel's milk will grow up to be strong. The way Demain saw it, any child would have to be strong to survive the stuff.

Even with the advent of chocolate flavoring, camel's milk is still not tremendously popular. For every gallon of camel's milk produced, almost 500 gallons of cow's milk are produced. There is another important thing about camel's milk; those who drink it tend to be extremely poor. Their lives and the lives of their camels are closely

71

intertwined. Those who milk camels don't tend to sell the milk. For the most part, camels' milk is entirely consumed by the tribes who own the camels. On rare occasions, rich Arabs do drink camel's milk. It is a luxury item that reminds them of their roots as poor desert-dwelling Bedouin. But that doesn't mean they actually like the stuff.

Demain thought that it was pretty funny that somebody overseas would be buying camel's milk. He'd tried it. It didn't kill him, but he thought it might. Nonetheless, he had his orders and he knew the facts. Eighty percent of all camel's milk was produced in Somalia because people in Somalia were too poor to drink anything else. Now, those same poor people were selling the milk. Obviously they thought they could use the money to buy better-tasting alternatives. They weren't selling it oversees, not directly. They didn't have the contacts to pull it off. They had to be selling it to a trader in Somalia who was exporting it to an oversees buyer. The question was, who was the trader?

Demain could think of only two ways to find the trader. One approach was to find out if any particular tribe was becoming unusually rich. Demain thought that approach would be a waste of time. There were many illicit ways to become rich in Somalia. It would be almost impossible to sort out the drug dealers, slave merchants and terrorists from the milkmen. No, Demain needed another approach. As he stood there, sweltering in the bazaar, Demain knew what he had to do.

He had to ask the camels themselves.

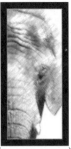

(SHORT EDDY)

An Elephant in the Park

It was so cool to walk Sam to my neighborhood. At first he was a little nervous. Well, actually, he was simultaneously nervous *and* excited. It was really really funny when he tried crawling along like he had the night before. I told him people might not notice an elephant, but they would certainly notice a belly-walking elephant. After a moment, he stood up a little sheepishly and started walking normally. We walked for a while and then I got tired. After all, I'd biked all the way to Northwest and I don't really like walking. So guess what? Sam actually kneeled and helped me climb up onto his neck. He then carried me the rest of the way.

We walked straight through downtown. Sure, people stared at us, but as I expected, they actually stared at me more than at him. They'd seen elephants; they'd never seen little kids riding elephants. I think some of them thought we were part of a movie. With some of the attention diverted from himself, Sam's gait slowly began to loosen up.

I remember we were striding along when I saw this one guy. He was maybe 40 and dressed in a business suit. He was walking really really fast talking on his cell phone and looking all-important. He was also carrying a very expensive briefcase. I first noticed him from like a block away. He was just charging up the street, obviously feeling very important. People jumped out of his way like he was an out of control cab. And he just kept going. He almost knocked over one little old lady and he didn't even apologize. I didn't like him very much. On the spot, I named him Mr. Pompous. The funny thing was, while I expected Mr. Pompous to ignore most people, I didn't expect him to not even notice Sam. I mean, Sam is pretty big. When Mr. Pompous got close to us, Sam tried to get out of his way. But there weren't many options. He didn't really want to crush an entirely innocent car. So, instead, Mr. Pompous just walked straight into Sam. And then Mr. Pompous just fell down. His cell phone dropped out of his hand and just like that he stopped talking. He was absolutely stunned to suddenly see a giant elephant standing right over him. It was then that I recognized him. It was Mean Eyes Paine's dad! I leaned down from Sam's neck and said, "Sorry Mister Paine, we tried to get out of the way, but you didn't see us."

He looked up, still very much in shock. Then he gathered up his brief case and his cell phone and he said, "Uh ... yeah." He seemed really uncertain. He was shaking his head like he had just seen a really weird vision as he walked away. He kept looking back at us to see if we were actually really real. He was looking our way when another little old lady tripped him with her cane. Poor Mr. Paine.

Our biggest problem wasn't people staring at us. Our biggest problem was fitting on the sidewalk. I'm pretty small and I don't take up much sidewalk. Because of that, I'd never imagined that sidewalks could be too small – especially the big sidewalks like those downtown. Sam, for his part, had never traveled in crowded places like this. Normally the sidewalk was even big enough for him. So, he didn't know what to do either. Basically, elephants are pretty big and sidewalks are actually pretty small – especially once you stick a bunch of people on them. As we walked, we were pushing lots of people out of the way. It wasn't a nice situation. After a while we decided to give up on the sidewalk and walk on the road. We figured we'd be less of a bother there. The problem was, we just barely squeezed into a lane.

At first, the cars were passing us very very quickly. But as we got further downtown, the traffic slowed. And then ... you guessed it ... we got caught in a traffic jam. You see, we were too big to walk around the cars and not quite big enough to safely step over them – especially when they kept stopping and starting unexpectedly. So we had to go with the flow of the cars.

Believe me, it was pretty weird sitting on an elephant's neck in the middle of downtown traffic, lurching forward and stopping and lurching forward and stopping just like I would have been doing had my mom been driving her car. But what were we supposed to do? We couldn't really fit on the sidewalk and we couldn't pass the cars. Because of that, getting through downtown took forever, but eventually the traffic cleared. And then, so did the sidewalks. We got back off to the side of the road and kept walking. We were both very happy to have downtown behind us.

Eventually we got to my neighborhood, where the park was. You know how some parks are like a block long and a block wide? Well, this park was really nice. It was like 6 blocks long and 4 blocks wide. It was a giant park. It had a baseball field, a pond, basketball courts, two playgrounds (one for bigger kids) and lots and lots of grass. It was a pretty fun place to hang out. When we got there, I kept Sam on the leash. It wasn't because I wanted to, it was just because all the parents were looking at him. They seemed worried that he'd walk on their children. I wasn't worried, but they were. So the leash stayed on. Even so, Sam had this dopey grin on his face. Normally those same parents would have called animal control. But because I was holding him, Sam had got to come to the park. Sam turned to me and said, "Thanks Eddy. I love goin' to parks. And this one seems real nice."

"You're welcome," I said. "Is there anything in particular you like to do at the park?"

"Naw," he responded, "I just like to sit on the grass and watch the people walk by. Some day I'd like to do a cannonball in a park pond, but I think it'd probably hurt the ducks."

"It probably would," I said, agreeing as I pictured ducks flying unwillingly through the air, propelled by Sam's giant splash. I was still thinking about that when Sam said, "Eddy, thanks for taking me here. I didn't know at first if I actually wanted to talk to you. I'm a little nervous around new people. But I guess my friend was right."

I thought, what friend? I didn't know about any friend. Sam hadn't told me about any friend. When I met him, Sam seemed to have no idea who I was. But when I thought about it, Sam was actually trying to be friendly. He did bring the park up out of the blue. It seemed weird at the time, but now I understood it.

"What friend?" I asked. I was very curious.

"Oh, nobody you know. He's just a little fella. He told me you'd visit and then you did. And he said you were a nice kid, and you were. He's a smart guy."

Now I was really intrigued. Who could possibly know that I'd visit Sam the elephant? Only one name came to mind – Thursday the Penguin. "Uh, Sam," I asked, "was it Thursday who said I'd visit?"

Sam had a sorta surprised look on his face. "How do you know about Thursday?" he asked, suspiciously.

And then it was my turn to fess up. Sure, Sam hadn't told me that he'd known I was coming, but I hadn't told him how I followed him home. "Sam," I said, "I met Thursday yesterday. I followed him to your secret meeting with him and then I followed you home."

"Oh," said Sam, "I know you followed me home. But I didn't know you knew Thursday. He's a funny little guy isn't he? But he isn't the friend I'm talking about."

"Yes," I said, agreeing that a little tiny bird in a trench coat was indeed funny. "But, Sam," I asked, "If it wasn't Thursday, who was it?"

Sam stared out towards the pond, "It is a very nice day isn't it."

"Sam?" I pushed.

And then he looked at me. "Listen, Eddy, I'm sorry I mentioned my friend. I can't tell ya about him because his identity is super secret. That okay?"

I could see that Sam was genuinely sorry he couldn't tell me more about his friend. So I said, "Fine. That's fine. Why don't you tell me how you came to be an elephant who lives in a warehouse in Northwest?"

Sam smiled and said, "Now that I can do. Let's see. I was born in a zoo. Actually in the Lakedale Zoo."

I was a bit confused; the Lakedale Zoo didn't have any elephants.

"Now I know what you're thinking," continued Sam. "The Lakedale Zoo doesn't have any elephants. Well, actually, it used to. It had elephants when I was born there. There were three of us – my mom, my dad and me. Now my mom and dad were perfect show elephants. They loved being on display and they loved kids looking and pointing at them. But for as long as I can remember, I hated it. I dreamed of nothing but leaving. My parents knew I wanted out. They knew they'd miss me when I left, but they also knew I simply wasn't happy in the Zoo.

"So, one night, my mom came upon the zookeeper's keys. She woke me up, opened the gate and said 'Sam, it's gonna be hard out there but I know you want to go. Your dad and I love you and will miss you terribly. Take care of yourself.'

"'I will,' I said, crying.

77

"Then my mom leaned real close to me and said, 'And, Sam, chase your dreams. They will make everything else worthwhile.'

"'I love you too, Mom' I said. And with that, I turned and left. Nobody saw me go. Nobody aside from my mom that is. I was scared of being seen, even more than usual. See, now they were looking for me and if they found me they'd take me back to the Zoo. While I would've loved to have seen my mom again, I couldn't go back to the Zoo. I had to stay out of sight. The problem was, I also had to eat. If it hadn't been for a mutual friend of ours I woulda starved in those early days."

"Who?" I asked, really interested in knowing. "Who helped you?"

"None other than Thursday," Sam continued. "He found me someplace to hide and got me regular clandestine shipments of peanuts and other foods. Elephants eat a lot, as I'm sure you know, and he made it possible for me to survive. He even set me up with a job at the junkyard crushing cars. It was a tough time for me. I never got to eat quite enough, but it was my first step in becoming an independent elephant."

"Are you okay now?" I asked.

"Ah," he said, "that's where my other friend, the one I can't tell you about, comes in. A couple of years later, he got me work and it pays better than the car crushing. Nowadays, I actually own a whole farm. And a family works on it for me. I pay 'em pretty well and they keep my pantry stocked up. It's a very nice arrangement. But, you see, there is still one huge problem."

"What?" I asked, genuinely wanting to be of help.

"I didn't do the one thing my mom told me to. I haven't chased my dreams. I mean, sure, I live well, I have a nice pad. But I never chased my dreams, not for real."

I had to ask, "Sam, what are your dreams?"

And then he told me one of the coolest things I had ever heard.

"I want to build an elephant city."

An elephant city!?! It took me a moment, but soon enough I could picture it; huge apartment blocks built on stocky foundations with elephants walking to and fro carrying giant bags of groceries. Pretty neat stuff. That was my picture, anyway. "What kind of elephant city?" I asked.

"Well..." said Sam bashfully, "It is all a little silly. I mean I don't even know that elephants would want to live in a city. So it is best that I just keep doin' what I'm doin'."

"But an elephant city is a great idea!" I enthused. "Tell me more about it!"

"You really want to know?" said Sam.

"Absolutely," I said.

"Why?" he asked.

"Because it is a super cool idea."

"Ok," said Sam, a big smile beginning to grow on his face. "Well, basically, I want to build an elephant city. I want elephant-sized houses and elephant-sized cafeterias and elephant-sized movie theaters and most of all I want elephant-sized swimming pools. You may have heard that elephants have great memories. Well, we're pretty smart in other ways too. So I figured we could do all sorts of neato jobs. We could be elephant lawyers and elephant doctors. Of course, some of us would be elephant firemen or elephant construction workers or just plain elephant moms and dads. And, like I said, we'd live in a city just like Lakedale, but for elephants. We wouldn't be afraid to be noticed or pointed out or picked on, because pretty much everybody would be an elephant. I mean, we'd let other people live there, but bottom line it would be our home. We'd even have super-wide sidewalks and grocery stores with monster aisles. It would be so neat." Sam was practically glowing as he said this last bit.

I had to admit, the elephant had a pretty good imagination. An elephant city. A place elephants could call home and live together with everything built for them. It was an excellent idea. I wanted to know more. So I asked, "How are you going to build it?"

And then, BAM!, just like that, all the excitement was gone. "I don't know," said Sam, a frown spreading across his face. "That's why the idea is stupid."

"Now wait," I said. "That doesn't mean it is stupid. That just means you don't know how to build it. Keep thinking about it and keep talking about it and it will come to you."

"Will it, Eddy? I don't really know. It just seems so far from here to there."

"It isn't far, Sam, not really. You can do it. Hey, I may not be an elephant, but you've got my vote of support already. I'll help out as much as I can. How many other people have you told?" I asked.

"None," said Sam. "I was afraid they'd laugh."

"Laugh? Why?"

"Because, Eddy," said Sam, "it's silly."

I could see we were going around in circles. So I changed the subject.

"Sam," I said, "do you have many friends?"

"Not many," he said. "I'm pretty nervous around new people."

"I don't have many friends either," I replied, sympathetically. "People may think you're strange because you're an elephant. But they think I'm strange because, well, I don't know why. My best friend in my whole life was my dad. Next is my mom, although she's more of a mom than a friend. And then there's you. But I don't have any other friends."

"That's too bad," said Sam. "The other kids are missing out on somethin'. But I have to tell you a secret."

"What?" I asked.

"You have many, many more friends than you know."

80

I didn't know what he was talking about, so I asked, "What do you mean?"

And Sam said, quietly, "I can't tell you exactly. But don't worry about having friends. You're a cool kid and a good kid and lots and lots of people like you, even love you."

I didn't know what to say. Sometimes it seemed like the elephant and his phantom friends knew more about me than I did. But I knew, once again, that Sam wasn't divulging any secrets. He might have a great memory, but he wasn't sharing it all with me.

"So, Eddy," said Sam, "thanks for taking me to the park. I was wondering. Can I see where you live?"

"Sure," I said. I grabbed his leash and we headed back out onto the street. You should have seen people's faces as we walked by. They weren't used to seeing elephants on the street. When we got to my place, the elephant tried to innocently shove a note into the fence. I pretended not to notice, although I wanted to grab the note and read it. Then Sam said, "That's a nice house. I'm afraid I can't fit in it." He sorta giggled at this last bit.

"No, I'm afraid you can't." I said.

"I guess I'll go home then," said Sam.

"Do you want me to walk you?" I asked.

"Naw," he said. "I'll head around the city this time. I just can't go to the park without you, because otherwise people get too scared."

"I understand," I said.

"Thanks, Eddy. I had a lotta fun today."

"You're welcome." He was welcome. Very welcome; I'd had a lot of fun too.

With that, Sam the Elephant – my friend – turned and walked away.

I looked at my watch. It was almost 3 o'clock. It was time to go see Thursday.

81

I was going to go home first, and get a quick drink. But when I turned around, there he was. Thursday was standing right in front of me. He was eating ice cream. I guessed that I wouldn't have to pay for admission to the water park.

I looked down at the little guy (remember he's only a foot tall) and said, "I thought I was going to meet you at your headquarters?"

Thursday slipped the ice cream back into his trench coat (I have no idea how it didn't wreck the thing) and responded, "I changed the plan."

"Ok," I said, excited about meeting him again. Little did I know that my excitement was only going to last a few seconds longer.

Thursday was looking pretty serious and determined. "Eddy, the spy game isn't for tykes. Don't follow me anymore." Thursday cleared his throat before adding the last bit, "I don't want to regret not giving you the forgetting drug." The little guy could be pretty threatening. I would have laughed him off, but that little bird was a whole lot tougher than he looked.

"Okay," I said, not having much choice. "I'll stop following you." It had been fun to play spy, but it wasn't really that important.

Thursday continued, "You also need to stop talking to the elephant."

"What?" I almost shouted. "Why can't I talk to Sam?"

"This is hurting me more than it is hurting you, Eddy. It is important to stop talking to him. The elephant is a critical intelligence asset and what he has to say is none of your business. You must stop talking to him."

"No!" I said, angry. "The elephant is my friend. I won't stop talking to him."

Thursday looked at me for a moment. Then, in a complete deadpan, he said, "Then I will drug you while you are sleeping and you will forget that he, or I, ever existed."

Thursday was completely serious.

I made my choice quickly. "Okay. Fine. If you want it that way, I will stop talking to the elephant. But it's not fair."

"I'm sorry, Eddy. But it's for your own good."

Moments later Thursday disappeared into the bushes.

I already missed my big gray friend.

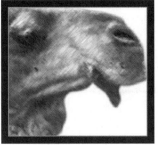

(NARRATOR)

Hadid the Camel

Demain was an excellent agent. There was just no question of that. When Demain made his decision to talk to the camels, it didn't involve starting from scratch and asking around until he had the answers he wanted. No. Instead, Demain, in his first three months on the job, had already cultivated an excellent camel informant. The camel's name was Hadid and he was a camel among camels.

Humans tend to think that Bedouin, those dusty camel-riding Arabs, are the soul of the desert. Those humans would be wrong. Not to dismiss the Bedouin, but the real knowledge and intelligence in the desert actually lays with the camels. Let's take an example. A group of Bedouin are riding across the North African desert. They are going from Abu-Alad to Alad-Abu. They've been riding for a few days when an argument starts. Mohammed, one Bedouin on a camel, feels that they are 3/4 of the way to Alad-Abu while Hafez, another Bedouin on a camel, thinks they are 2/3 of the way.

Mohammed says, "We are 3/4 of the way. Sure, we've only been riding for 3 days, but the camels have been going faster than usual."

"No!" retorts Hafez, thumping his leg. "We are 2/3 of the way! The camels have been going slower than usual and we've only been riding for 2 and a half days." A tremendous argument ensues.

What neither man knows, but both their camels do know, is that they have traveled exactly 17/24ths of the way to Alad-Abu. And how do the camels know this? Because camels find long trips extremely boring. To pass the time, they count their footsteps. Every camel knows it is 25,673 average steps from Abu-Alad to Alad-Abu and every camel in that caravan knew that they had traveled 18,182 footsteps so far. So while their riders argued, the camels trudged along, snorting at human stupidity. You might think that it doesn't require much intelligence to count your footsteps, but you would be completely wrong. We humans only have two legs. Counting steps with two legs is easy. But camels have four legs – four legs constantly in motion. You'd probably have a hard time counting 25,673 steps with just your two legs. But imagine doing it with four legs! It isn't easy. From this we can see that camels have excellent concentration and counting skills. But there's more. You see, those 25,673 footsteps are *average* footsteps and not one camel in that group was quite average. Not only were the camels counting their footsteps (and not losing count), they were averaging all their results during the entire trip. When you have 19 camels in a caravan, averaging footsteps can be a real mental challenge. In case you didn't know, averaging the footsteps of 19 camels requires adding all those steps together and then dividing by 19 – all without losing count of your own footsteps. And camels, while smart, don't have calculators. They have to do all these calculations in their head. Why do camels bother with it? As explained earlier, they find long trips very very boring. Counting and averaging provides at least some entertainment.

Demain, during his three months of operations in Somalia, had created a tremendously strong relationship with one particularly intelligent and well-informed camel, Hadid. Hadid knew everything.

Hadid had been on every caravan route, Hadid had hung out with lots of different groups of Bedouin. As Hadid put it, he was on a first name basis with half the camels in North Africa. Hadid had it all figured out. Why was this particular camel so well informed?

Simple.

Hadid hated people. So whenever he had the chance, he spat at them. Because his disposition was so bad, he kept getting sold to different groups of unsuspecting Bedouin. Most camels with his attitude would have been eaten, but Hadid was in top physical form and thus worth quite a bit more alive than dead.

Demain, while sneaking around in the bazaar, had noticed Hadid the camel. Demain saw, immediately, that Hadid had this incredibly observant look about him. He was just the type of camel who you knew had a lot of information stored in his head. So Demain struck up a conversation. Demain wanted information and he was willing to pay to get it. He wanted to see what the camel knew and what he wanted in return. After a little probing, he got his answer. Hadid knew everything, and he would tell Demain anything he wanted to know as long as he was sufficiently compensated with bottles of fruit cordial.

Fruit cordial?

Yes, fruit cordial. The liquid stuff you add to water that flavors it. For camels, Blackberry fruit cordial is a favorite choice.

Hadid's love for fruit cordial wasn't unusual. All camels like fruit cordial. In fact, all camels *really* like fruit cordial. To them, fruit cordial is like solid gold. It might seem strange, but it isn't. In fact, it is so logical that you might slap yourself for not understanding it straight away. If you do slap yourself, please don't do it too hard. Your mom might get angry with me.

Camels carry water around for weeks at a time. After that kind of time in a camel tank, even water can get pretty stale. Over a thousand years ago, a famous camel named Ahmed drank back a small bottle of Chinese cordial he found in a Arabian bazaar. As the famous story goes, Ahmed was delighted with the result. The stale water he was carrying around in his hump suddenly tasted fresh and full of flavor. It was so much nicer than normal water had been. From that time onwards, camels have loved fruit cordial more than anything else on earth.

That day, when Demain went to visit Hadid, he just happened to have a few extra bottles of fruit cordial stashed in his pack. All he wanted in return for the precious liquid was a little information. He wanted Hadid to tell him who was buying up camel's milk. So, in his customarily confident fashion, he snuck over to the part of town where Hadid was living, sidled up next to him and asked, "Hadid, my old friend, you heard anything interesting?" Now, Demain wasn't Hadid's friend and Hadid wasn't Demain's friend. They just talked that way when doing business. If not for the fruit cordial, Hadid would have spat (or even sat) on Demain. If not for the information, Demain would have ignored Hadid as a lowly camel. But they needed each other, and so they talked like friends. Perhaps they both thought such behavior would lend them an advantage in negotiations.

"Sure," said Hadid. "I heard that a certain warlord is gathering weapons for an assault in the north. He thinks the competition down here in the south is too fierce. I'll give you his name for a bottle."

"Ah," said Demain, "sorry, I'm not interested in that. I was more curious about something involving camel's milk?"

"Camel's milk?" said Hadid, "Why would you care?"

"Well I just heard somebody was out buying camel's milk for export, a lot of it. I thought you might know something about it."

"I do," said Hadid, "but it will cost you. Normally information this important would cost four bottles, but today, because you are such a special friend, I will only charge you two."

Four bottles of fruit cordial was a princely sum. Two bottles was only a slightly less princely sum.

"But Hadid," said Demain, "I only have one bottle with me. For a friend like you I would be glad to pay two bottles for such information, but I can't."

"There are solutions to such problems," said Hadid. "You pay me one now, and then you pay me one later."

"Hadid, my old friend, that sounds like a deal." Demain actually had three bottles of fruit cordial on him, but he wasn't going to tell the camel that. It was hard to get the stuff in Somalia and he wanted to get as much information for it as he possibly could. He also didn't want the camel to get too greedy.

Demain handed over one of his three bottles and then Hadid starting talking. "Okay, Here's the story. There's a company called The Stringy Teet based in Bender Cassim. They are located right on the harbor. They are buying up loads of camel's milk and freezing it. Nobody knows why, but it is a big-time operation up there." Hadid paused, but only for a little bit, "So, when do I get that second bottle of cordial?"

Hadid had told Demain exactly what he needed to know. So Demain said, "I'll go home and get it now."

The camel said, "I look forward to your return. As always, it is a pleasure doing business with you."

"It has been a pleasure to do business with you as well," said Demain. And it had been a pleasure. For an ambitious penguin like Demain, Hadid's words were solid gold. Demain had received his first mission and he was carrying it out in record time. He could already smell the commendation.

As Demain pretended to head home for the second bottle of cordial, he dreamed of climbing the ranks at PENGUIN.

(NARRATOR)

A Moment of Clarity

Grobar's home was an abandoned Cold-War-era heavy water production plant. It wasn't just any cold war heavy water production plant though. It was an abandoned *underground* heavy water production plant. The place was huge, but on the surface there was almost no indication that it even existed. It was the kind of thing that only Grobar would have noticed. The goat happened to be pouting his way across the plains when he came across a squat phone-booth looking thing. He touched a button on it, and a second later a door opened. Naturally curious, Grobar walked through the door and was whisked downward by a very fast elevator. A door at the bottom opened and Grobar found himself in a long hallway with sets of doors on either side and what looked like a group of old aluminum cans. Just like that, Grobar realized that he had found his new home.

Grobar didn't live alone in this heavy water production plant. No, the plant came with a cutting edge security system (well, it was cutting edge during the Cold War). The aluminum cans were security robots. They became the only family Grobar had.

Family or not, Grobar didn't like the robots much. They seemed to be more trouble than they were worth. And, being pretty old, they weren't exactly the most reliable things around. Nonetheless, Grobar tolerated them and lived in relative peace and solitude beneath the vast plains of his homeland.

When Grobar got the recipe for the mind control potion from the Queen Ant (back before he knew he wanted to take over the world), he decided to go home and try it out immediately.

While the Queen Ant had a Flying Ant Service to get her ingredients, there was no Flying Goat equivalent. The aerodynamics didn't work out. This meant that Grobar needed to actually buy the ingredients for the mind control drug on the open market. Luckily, there were a few valuable things lying around the old heavy water plant – things like weapons-grade plutonium. Grobar made a few bucks selling the stuff. He then spent many fewer bucks buying all the ingredients he needed. Finally, as you tend to do when you want to experiment with a mind control potion, Grobar (who had become a very mean goat) abducted a test subject. The test subject happened to be a nice young local man named Altan. After mixing the ingredients (and tying down Altan), Grobar tried out the recipe for the first time – forcing Altan to drink it.

The drug didn't work. Altan tasted it and said, "Yummy."

That annoyed Grobar, but he had plenty of time on his hands, so he started trying different variations. He substituted Arabian camel's milk for Somalian camel's milk, he tried Vermont State apples instead of Washington State apples and he even tried Chinese kiwis instead of New Zealand kiwis. But nothing worked. For months and months, Grobar labored. Every time he forced Altan to drink the drug, the young man just said, "Yummy."

Grobar was getting nowhere.

Finally, because he had it handy, Grobar replaced the regular water in the recipe with heavy water that happened to be laying around.

One sip by his human guinea pig (just remember never to call a real guinea pig a guinea pig, they find it demeaning), and Grobar found himself controlling Altan as if he was an ant. With a thought, Grobar could see what Altan saw and make Altan do anything Grobar wanted. When Grobar didn't want to control Altan any more, he just stopped – and Atlan remembered nothing. He didn't even remember to say, "Yummy."

Grobar thought that was pretty cool.

So he captured more human subjects. And because he figured they might be useful for some reason, he sent them all over the place. He kept Altan at home, just in case he needed him. It wasn't long before Grobar had operatives from America to Africa to Afghanistan.

When Grobar did finally decide to take over the world, he tried for months and months to come up with a decent plan. He already had everything laying right in front of him. He had a mind control potion; he had agents all over the world; he even had a secret lair – all that he needed to do was put it all together. When he shouted, "Ah ha, I've got it!" and then proceeded to dictate his entire plan to his computer (in front of Bartholomew), all he did was finally figure out that he could use the queen ant's mind control potion to control *everybody*.

This simple, curious and lonely goat *was very close to taking over the world*.

(SHORT EDDY)

A Missing Bike

I wasn't happy about my meeting with Thursday. Fine, I could understand he was worried about me, but what was wrong with me talking to Sam? Sam and I really got along and Sam was my friend. But I had promised Thursday, and I don't break my promises. I wouldn't talk to Sam.

Dejected, I walked into my house and straight into the kitchen. I was going to fix myself a hot chocolate and then I was going to go upstairs and play on my computer. I didn't know what else to do. I had just poured the milk into my cup when my mom walked in. She asked, "Did you have a nice day, Eddy?" I didn't know what to say; I'd had a great day until about five minutes earlier. So I said, in a very dejected voice, "Yeah."

"What's wrong?" asked my Mom.

"You don't want to know," I said. And I meant it. It would only upset my mom if I told her about Sam.

"I think I would like to know," said my Mom.

And that was it; I didn't have a choice. So the whole story just sorta spilled out of me. I told her about how I went to Northwest to meet Sam and about how we became friends and about how

Thursday made me promise not to talk to him. And do you know what my mom did? She got out her little notebook, just like she always does, and she started writing in it. And then she asked, "Eddy, did you leave your bike at Sam's?"

My mom was pretty smart. She had been listening to my story – even if she didn't seem to believe a word of it. So I said, "Yeah. I'm sorry."

With her voice full of motherly disapproval she stated, "I think you'd better go get it."

I responded, almost whining, "But I can't, I promised Thursday."

"It's okay," she said, concern in her voice. "You don't have to talk to Sam, you just have to get your bike. I'll drive you up to Northwest and drop you off and you can come home later. Is that okay?"

Now, you've got to admit it was a weird offer. Why would my mom, who didn't believe my stories, be willing to drive me up to Northwest to get a bike I had left in a warehouse she didn't believe existed It was all pretty hard to understand. She was probably playing that weird psychology game and endulging my fantasy world so it would go away. But the fact was, I had left my bike at Sam's and I did need to get it. Plus, my mom was offering me a ride to Northwest. It would have taken me forever to walk there. So I just said, "Ok Mom, I'd love a ride up to Sam's."

"Fine," she said, "I'll just go get my keys."

My mom was so cool.

In about five minutes we were on the road. My mom, even though she's a normal boring adult, drives a pretty neat car. Because it's just the two of us, she doesn't need anything big like a minivan, so she drives this 1972 Jaguar E-type convertible. It is a long, low slung, and very nice looking car. My mom calls it sexy. Whenever we drive it, we get a lot of looks. My mom, although a normal mom in most respects, loves cars. She told me that I used to ride in the tiny back seat of the Jaguar when I was a kid and my dad was around. Whenever she tells me about it she gets this misty tone in her voice. She loved it when there were three of us in that car.

We drove north, sticking to the freeways that went around downtown. Even without my dad, I still loved cruising along the freeway with the top down and the wind blowing through my hair. The car doesn't have a very good radio, so my mom always leaves it off. When we drive, it is just the two of us, driving the road and enjoying the feel of the wind. Occasionally my mom will reach over and give my shoulder a squeeze. I like that.

We got to Sam's pretty quickly, my mom driving and me pointing the way. My mom seemed to trust me implicitly. When I got out of the car and said "Goodbye" she just sped away waving her hand happily.

And then there I was, in the middle of Northwest, in the middle of the street, about to visit the one person I had promised Thursday I wouldn't talk to.

Just to make sure, I checked the junkyard for my bike. It wasn't there. Being a nice elephant, Sam must have brought it inside.

I walked up to Sam's door and slid it open. I couldn't talk to Sam, so I didn't bother knocking or saying my name or anything. The door was very well greased and it opened soundlessly. I slipped inside and then looked up to see where Sam was. It was then that I saw him.

No, not Sam, someone else.

Somebody quite a bit smaller. A frog actually. Yup, a small frog – probably the same kind you can never find when you go to the Zoo and look in the little boxes, was sitting on a table in the middle of Sam's room. He was turned to face the elephant, who was making dinner, and neither of them had noticed me.

When I closed the door behind myself, it made a clanging noise. In that instant, both the frog and Sam turned to see me. It was the frog who spoke first, "My name's Bartholomew, Bartholomew the Frog with Precision Hopping Ability. And I've been expecting you."

Expecting me? How had he been expecting me? Keeping in mind my promise to Thursday, I didn't say a word.

Bartholomew continued, "I know about your promise to Thursday. And, you have to keep it. Sam also knows about your promise; he won't be insulted if you don't say 'hello.' But you can say 'hello' to me. Thursday said nothing about not talking to a small, very rare, frog."

He was right, Thursday hadn't said anything about a frog. So I said, "Hello, Bartholomew."

"It is a pleasure to meet you formally," said Bartholomew. "I knew your father. He was my mentor and everything I do is guided by the advice he gave me. I've also known you for many years. That is why, despite Thursday's fears, I am going to tell you about Grobar the Goat."

I was confused. Who was Grobar the Goat and what did my father have to do with a goat and this frog. And how had this frog known me for years and years.

"My father?" I asked, pulling together the single most important question I had. "Is he alive?"

"We think so," said Bartholomew. "But we don't know where he is."

I wanted to hear more about my dad, but before I could gather any more of my thoughts, Bartholomew interjected, "I can tell you more about your father, later. But now we have a problem to fix. We have to deal with Grobar the Goat."

I was still standing there, stunned, when I heard myself say, "Okay."

For the next ten minutes, Bartholomew told me about the case of Grobar the Goat.

I listened, and I understood, but I was only really thinking about one thing – this frog knew something about my father.

(NARRATOR)

Container City

Demain got Hadid his bottle of cordial in record time. It helped that he was just pretending to head home for something that was already in his backpack. He couldn't wait to head north, to Bender Cassim. His mission was almost over. After delivering the cordial, Demain rushed back to his own office in a particularly seedy part of Mogadishu. As soon as he got there, he strapped himself into his personal fighter jet faster than you can say 'personal fighter jet.' Demain's personal fighter jet was just like Thursday's. It was a small jet airplane with advanced electronics, radar and weapons systems. But, standard PENGUIN issue personal fighter jets have a few additional features. One of these was its ability to fly both through the sky and under the water. Another was its vertical launch feature. Known as the P-480, the airplane could take off without any runway at all. It shot straight up into the air like a rocket. With a top airspeed of over Mach 1.5 and a top water speed of 90 knots, the P-480 was a PENGUIN field agent's ideal method of transportation.

After carrying out his pre-flight check, Demain slammed on the throttle and launched his small airplane straight into the air. Bender Cassim was less than an hour away.

For years, Bender Cassim had been a poor backwater in an already poor country. Then the government of Somalia fell and

Bender Cassim was changed forever. The city was suddenly independent. While the rest of Somalia sank into chaos, Bender Cassim took off. Bender Cassim, the poor Somalian backwater, had two things to its credit. One, it had a port. Two, it possessed a desperate desire to survive. Because of these things, Bender Cassim became a hub of trade. Once a town of 20,000, it grew to a small city of 100,000. People from throughout Somalia, and neighboring countries, moved to the blossoming city. Refugees from the rest of the country came flocking to its dusty streets. Bender Cassim represented hope in a near hopeless land. It was a place where business could be done. Bender Cassim, a city of traders, was by no means rich, but at least it wasn't collapsing.

As a place from which to export camel's milk, Bender Cassim was an obvious choice. It was peaceful, allowing for uninterrupted operations. And in Bender Cassim, nobody would notice the export of yet another agricultural commodity. However, the brains behind the export operation hadn't counted on the camels themselves talking about their operation. They hadn't counted on Hadid and his ilk. And they certainly hadn't expected Demain to be hanging out in Mogadishu, willing to buy whatever information Hadid was selling. Finally, they hadn't expected Demain to fly to Bender Cassim to pay their facility a little visit.

Demain reached Bender Cassim in less than an hour. It was, after all, only 700 miles away. In the interests of security, he dropped under water some 20 miles outside of town. He soon reached his destination, the port of Bender Cassim. Parking covertly, literally in the harbor, Demain opened the hatch on his P-480 and swam to the dockside. Stealthily, he surfaced right underneath the dock. The shadows of the ships and the dock wall completely cloaked his presence.

Demain reached into his pack and attached grappling hooks to his wings. He then swam along the dockside looking for the ladder he

knew he would find. Eventually, he found it. Carefully climbing –
hard work for a penguin – Demain stuck his head above the dock
wall and quickly scanned the waterfront. Nobody noticed him.
Demain hopped up onto the waterfront and ran in between two low-
slung buildings. Once again, the shadows covered him.

Demain detached his grappling arms. He was about to venture
back to the waterfront, from which he would have a better chance of
locating The Stringy Teet, when, by pure chance, he looked up.
There, plastered in the shadows, was a small sign. It read, "The
Stringy Teet."

Demain had reached his destination.

In order to circumvent any security the place might have,
Demain got out a small supersaw, another standard PENGUIN item.
Demain, whenever possible, didn't like to use doors or windows.
Alarm systems tended to concentrate on such places. Demain much
preferred entering facilities through their walls. It was standard
PENGUIN protocol and Demain executed it flawlessly. Pulling out
his supersaw, he furtively cut a penguin-sized hole in the side of the
Stringy Teet. In a moment he was through the hole and inside the
building.

When Demain looked around, he saw bank after bank of massive
freezer-enabled shipping containers. These special containers, each
40 feet long, ten feet tall and ten feet wide, are meant to carry goods
– frozen goods – on ships. They were ideal for shipping large
amounts of camel's milk. Demain briskly walked to the nearest of the
containers and climbed on top of it. There was a delivery address
there. It read:

Kidd Pharmaceuticals

280 NW Fremont

Lakedale, USA

Demain memorized the address. He knew where the containers
were headed. But he still didn't know if they were full of camel's

milk. Demain opened a small door on top of the container. He immediately knew he had found what he was looking for. There was an
off-white substance inside and it had a remarkably pungent odor.
Hadid had been right. He was in a room full of camel's milk. Frozen
camel's milk. It was disgusting.

Just then, Demain heard a noise. Somebody had come into the
room. Without a second's thought, Demain tossed himself through
the door and into the container. It was freezing cold. While most
people, or animals, would have disliked the chill, Demain had spent
a great deal of time in Antarctica. He found the cold quite comfortable. It was almost nostalgic. It was the smell that bothered him.
Unfortunately, penguins can't pinch their noses.

Listening carefully, Demain heard two voices talking.

The first voice, which belonged to a male with a lightly Asian
accent, said, "What quantities of white camel's milk have you here?"
The man was speaking in perfect Arabic. He was also speaking in a
remarkably robotic voice. Demain, of course, also spoke flawless
Arabic.

The second voice, which belonged to a male with a thick Somali
accent, responded, "My friend, 15,000 gallons of milk occupy each of
the containers before you. Taken together, the containers before you
hold no less than 225,000 gallons of camel's milk. Already, we have
accumulated a tenth of the lofty and worthy sum you seek."

"Good," said the first voice. "You will be rewarded handsomely.
Three dollars per gallon is the price we agreed to – and for rapid
delivery one dollar per gallon of bonus. If all is as it should be, you
will be paid all four dollars for each gallon."

"Thank you, my beneficent friend," said the second voice. "All is
as it should be and everything is as we agreed." Demain could hear
he was already counting the dollars. Like Demain himself, the

second voice had no idea what the milk was going to be used for. Then the first voice said something that actually scared Demain. It said, "Berke, Batu, examine the containers. Make sure everything is as it should be."

Immediately, Demain heard a shuffling of feet and the sound of hinges being swung open. Berke and Batu, whoever they were, were opening the containers! Demain knew it was only a matter of time before their found him. As a PENGUIN agent, he knew that being discovered would have been worse than failure. PENGUIN was, after all, super secret. So, containing his revulsion for the milk, Demain pulled out his supersaw. Sawing furiously, Demain cut his way through the frozen milk. He steered straight for the far end of the container. It was pushed up against an outside wall. As he worked, he heard one of the two thugs say, "Chinusuren, there's a noise. Somebody is here." His voice was also strangely robotic.

The first voice, which Demain could now identify as belonging to Chinusuren, responded flatly, "Find them."

Immediately, Demain heard footsteps running towards his container. Demain was almost at the far wall of the container when the opposite end of it swung open. Demain knew Berke and Batu couldn't possibly see him through all the milk. He also knew it would only be a matter of time before they could. Working furiously with his supersaw, he sliced through the last bit of frozen milk. The teeth on his saw bit into the side of the container. Thirty seconds more and he'd be out!

Batu or Berke, Demain didn't know which, said, "Chinusuren, they're in here."

Chinusuren answered, coolly, "Get them." His vocabulary seemed limited.

Although Demain couldn't see them, he could hear that both Batu and Berke had pulled out and chambered submachine guns. They started shooting through the milk-ice. The bullets couldn't reach Demain. Not yet. But they were breaking up the milk-ice awfully fast. It wouldn't be long before Demain was visible.

He couldn't let them discover him.

Demain got out his mini-bomb – a PENGUIN's weapon of last resort. The mini-bomb would incinerate a square city block, leaving nothing behind. Activating it would also activate explosive charges on his P-480 and his office in Mogadishu as well. Demain didn't activate it though. He just got it ready. Instead, he continued sawing furiously, the sounds of bullets chewing through ice-milk growing closer and closer. One of the thugs said, "I can see a rough shape." Demain knew it was almost over. He got ready to destroy all evidence of his existence, including himself.

Then, finally, he broke through the wall. He landed in the alley outside the building just as he heard Batu say, "Chinusuren, he disappeared." The voice still completely lacked emotion.

Running as quickly as a penguin can possibly run, Demain headed for the waterfront. He fell over once (penguins aren't very good at running), but he eventually made it. As he dove into the water, he heard the door on the The Stringy Teet's warehouse swing open. Nobody would have seen him, but they wouldn't have any problem guessing where he had gone. Crashing into the harbor, he headed straight for his P-480. He heard bullets cutting through the water above him. Chinusuren, Batu and Berke didn't see him, but they couldn't have missed where he splashed into the harbor. Luckily, he was already out of reach of both their bullets and their eyes.

Penguins might be slow on land, but they can swim pretty fast.

Before long, Demain had climbed into the hatch of his P-480. Only then did he put his mini-bomb away. Hitting the engines, he flew through the water, heading as far away from Bender Cassim as he could possibly get. After about 20 minutes, he pulled the nose of his little craft upwards. He surged through the surface and took to the sky. He turned his aircraft around and headed south, towards Mogadishu. Then, and only then, he let himself breathe a sigh of relief. It had been a very close encounter.

His mission wasn't complete though. As he flew, he broadcast an emergency message to PENGUIN HQ:

START TRANSMISSION

TARGET LOCATED.

KIDD PHARMACEUTICALS

280 NW FREMONT

LAKEDALE, USA

INFILTRATION DISCOVERED

AWAITING FURTHER ORDERS

END TRANSMISSION

And then, finally, his mission was complete. He wasn't so sure about a commendation. He hadn't managed to do what PENGUIN field agents are trained to do: get in and out of a target building without anybody ever knowing for sure that he had ever been there. Nonetheless, he had accomplished his mission.

And for that, he knew that Hadid deserved a bonus.

(NARRATOR)

Kidd Pharmaceuticals

Remember that Sam had stuck a secret note in the fence in front of Eddy's house? Remember that Thursday had picked it up? Well, that note contained Bartholomew's answer to PENGUIN's question, 'Did the mind control potion work?' The answer was short and to the point, the story of William McGrover confirmed that Grobar's drug worked and that Grobar was extremely dangerous. Thursday hadn't been there just to warn Short Eddy. He'd also been there for the note.

Knowing that the drug worked, Thursday radioed PENGUIN HQ. To his surprise, it wasn't long before they responded. They had an address which they believed housed Grobar's factory. It was 280 NW Fremont, in Lakedale itself. They wanted Thursday to investigate. If appropriate, they wanted him to mess it up.

Thursday hopped in his penguin-sized sports car and drove straight to the alleged factory.

At first glance, there was nothing unusual about the place. The building wasn't shabby and it wasn't nice. It was just a typical medium-sized industrial building. A sign outside announced that it was used by an outfit called Kidd Pharmaceuticals. The parking lot was full and Thursday could see people walking around inside. A truck was even backing up to the loading dock. The whole place looked very normal.

Thursday's little sports car, while very nice, doesn't just move him from point A to point B while absorbing the impact of random car tires (it is amazing how many people run over things they don't see). It is also loaded with surveillance equipment. A heads-up display and a superb speaker system are hooked up to high power telescopes, long-distance microphones and multi-spectrum cameras. The rig was stuffed with the kind of toys every PENGUIN agent liked to have around.

Flipping on the car's high-powered telescope, Thursday zoomed in on the unloading truck. What exactly was it carrying? It didn't take long to find out. It was stuffed to the brim with Washington Apples – one of Grobar's four secret ingredients. Suddenly, the innocent-looking building didn't seem so innocent anymore.

Investigating further, Thursday focused his long distance microphone and high-powered telescope on two men talking. He could see them through one of the building's windows. Maybe if he learned something about them he'd be able to figure out where Grobar was coming from. He couldn't tell though. The two men looked Asian, but they were speaking in a language that Thursday just couldn't place. It wasn't Chinese or Japanese. Thursday was watching them for five minutes, hoping for an insight. And then he saw the sign posted on the wall behind them. He zoomed in on it. It wasn't in English – instead, it was written in a beautifully flowing, and very unusual, script. Thursday didn't know what the language was. But he knew that if he could figure that out, he'd know where Grobar was from.

As the car had recorded everything Thursday had seen, he decided that he had enough evidence to solve the case. He just had to work through it. The time had come to mess things up.

Thursday hit the gas on his little car and headed up to a farm on the northern outskirts of Lakedale. This wasn't your normal farm. It didn't have cows and pigs or corn and wheat. Instead, it housed a most unusual business run by a hedgehog named Pierre. Pierre sold pests. He sold all sorts of pests, from annoying rats to annoying answering machine messages to the item Thursday came for that day – apple worms. Thursday bought a couple thousand worms from him and headed back to 280 NW Fremont.

As soon as he got back to the factory, Thursday tiptoed up to the loading dock. He didn't see anyone around, so he silently edged his way into the warehouse. It was dark inside, but even in the dark he could make out the giant pile of apples that seemed to fill the entire place. Quickly, Thursday untied the bags of worms and poured them out on the floor. Thursday backed up against a wall and watched as the worms headed for the apples. Just before the last worm disappeared under the pile, he turned back to Thursday and said, "Thanks for the treat, penguin dude!" Thursday just nodded and snuck back out of the building.

His mission was complete. Thursday hopped into his car and started driving home. He was chuckling to himself about the worms, when he suddenly realized what language the guys in the factory had been speaking.

It had been Mongolian.

He knew that because, back in spy school, he'd studied Genghis Khan's efforts to introduce a new Mongolian alphabet. Mr. Khan had come very close to taking over the world. He was one of the first world-conquering people PENGUIN had been called in to stop. Thursday didn't know why it was important for spies to know about Mr. Khan's alphabet, but it had been on the exam, so he learned it. Until that moment, driving home from Kidd Pharmaceuticals, he'd never had any use for the information. But at that moment, he was glad he'd learned it. If the guys in the factory were Mongolian, chances were high that Grobar was too. It kind of made sense. There are lots of goats in Mongolia.

Thursday punched the gas.

Mongolia was waiting.

(SHORT EDDY)

Cola, Coffee and Tea

I listened to the frog talk about Grobar. I listened, but I was really thinking about my dad. Even so, I did catch the basics; there was a power hungry goat and he was threatening to take over the world with a caffeine-activated mind-dominating drug. Apparently, the organization Thursday belonged to was trying to find this goat, but so far had only come up with a way of locating his factory.

After about ten minutes of listening to the story, I said to the frog, "This goat needs somebody who can distribute the drug in caffeine drinks."

"Like a distributor of caffeinated beverages?" asked Bartholomew.

"Sure," I said, "Like a distributor. If we could find a distributor we might just be able to find the goat."

The frog, Bartholomew, responded, "I've been looking for a distributor, but I haven't found anything."

I thought for a bit before responding, "Well, it must be either coffee, cola or tea. If I'm the goat and I want to quickly take over the world, my first choice would be cola. There are only really two important cola companies."

108

"Yup," said Bartholomew, "Grobar went straight for the cola companies. Remember, I found William McGrover was drugged. But he failed to get Grobar's initiative past the board of SodaCo. It is possible that he tried GoodDrinks, but I doubt he'd get much further with them."

"What," I asked, as Sam's head swung between the two of us, watching us talk, "About tea?"

"Well," said Bartholomew, with a smile, "tea used to be one of the standard tools for world domination. The British Empire was built on tea. But, today, lots of people in lots of countries produce it. I don't think Grobar could effectively take over the tea market. He certainly couldn't do it quickly."

"What if he went after the people who sell tea, like Wingers?" I asked.

Bartholomew, after a moment of thought, said, "No, that wouldn't work well either. You see, there are just too many tea distributors. Nobody has a big enough piece of the market for Grobar to be able to quickly have a real impact."

"That leaves coffee," I concluded.

"Yes," said the frog, "I got to the same place. The problem is, coffee is also hard to take over. Like tea, it is made all over the place – from Brazil to Colombia to Africa. And lots of people make it."

"Ah," I said, "but lots of people buy a morning coffee at a place like Drowning Donuts and La Republica. Perhaps, just maybe, somebody can influence the morning coffee companies?"

"Again," responded Bartholomew, speaking with the authority that came with knowledge, "it doesn't quite work that way. I think they would run into the same problems that McGrover of SodaCo did. Normal companies aren't so easy to take over."

We both sat and thought for a bit, trying to figure out what Grobar's next move would be. Then, suddenly, a thought came into my head, "What if Grobar tried to strike in between the two? What if, instead of going after the growers and instead of going after the morning coffee companies, he went after the distributors that sold Drowning Donuts their beans?"

The frog pondered my idea, "Hmmm.... That's a possibility. The three biggest chains are all supplied by only two distributors: BeanInc and CoffeeCorp. Both of those companies are based in Colombia. Perhaps, just maybe, Grobar could strike up an alliance with the Colombian drug lords who could then force those companies to spike the coffee they sell."

"Can we find out if he's doing that?" I asked.

"Absolutely!" exclaimed Bartholomew.

Before he made any phone calls or anything, I wanted to ask him more about my dad. "Bartholomew, before you do anything else, can you tell me a little more about my dad?"

"I can only tell you about your dad," said Bartholomew, "but I can't tell you lots about what he did. I know he loves you and your mom more than anything in the world. I know he is an incredible man. He is brilliant, he is good, and he is wise. Your dad taught me, and he guided me, but he never said much about himself. He did important work, he was helping the world in some incredible ways, but I don't know exactly how. Before he disappeared, he did tell me that he was in some kind of trouble. But he didn't know much. He was just worried. That's why he left you the Gryffin. He didn't have time to teach you how to use it. But I think he hoped that you would eventually use it."

"Can you teach me how to use the Gryffin?"

"I'm sorry, Eddy," responded Bartholomew, "but I can't. I just don't know enough about it."

"We'll, I'd like whatever help you can give me," I said, optimistically.

Bartholomew hopped on my shoulder, like he was trying to give me a reassuring, friendly, hug. "Let me go check out the drug lord's angle." he said. "Afterwards, I'll give you all the help I possibly can."

"Okay," I responded.

And then he did the weirdest thing ever. He leaned back like he was about to hop off my shoulder and then he just hopped – and disappeared! Yes, you heard me right. He disappeared. Vanished. Nothing to see here folks! The frog was gone. Sam looked at me. He saw how confused I was.

He couldn't talk to me, because of my promise to Thursday, so he grabbed a pen and some paper with his trunk and wrote, 'Bartholomew isn't a normal frog.'

That, I knew. Nonetheless, I smiled at Sam. I was glad to have him as a friend even if I couldn't talk to him. As the silence stretched on, we both sat there, sharing the same room and not talking.

We were both just waiting for the little green, very rare, frog to return.

(SHORT EDDY)

Colombian Grown

It seemed like Bartholomew took forever to get back. When he did, he just popped right in view. One second there was an empty table, the next there was a frog sitting there.

It was a little weird.

"You were right," said the frog, speaking to me. "The drug lords are getting involved. They aren't there yet, but it's real close."

"Where'd you go?" I asked.

"To the drug lords," Bartholomew said, as if it were the most natural thing in the world.

"Huh?" I asked, very confused.

"I'll explain it later," said Bartholomew, "But we have to call Thursday right now. Sam, call him on his cell phone and let him know that Grobar is having a meeting with some Colombian drug lords at his headquarters. The drug lords are leaving Medellin in 30 minutes and heading to the 45th parallel via Tripoli."

Sam hit the speakerphone with his trunk. He had Thursday on speed dial. A second later, Thursday picked up, "Thursday here."

"Thursday?" said Sam.

"What do you need?" asked the penguin.

"Thursday, good buddy, 'The Source' has more information on Grobar."

"What is it?" asked Thursday.

"Grobar is havin' a meeting with some Colombian drug lords from Medellin at his headquarters. We know that these headquarters are located along the 45th parallel, probably somewhere east of Tripoli. The drug lords are going to leave Medellin in about 30 minutes. We think they're goin' to fly via Tripoli."

"Thanks, Sam," Thursday said. "I'll head to the far east right now. I hope we can figure out exactly where Grobar is located once I get there."

"Sounds good, old buddy," responded Sam, happily, "although I want some really nice nuts when you get back."

"Absolutely, Sam, how about some Brazil nuts?"

"That sounds great!" rumbled the jovial elephant.

"Consider it done," Thursday said. "Over and out."

Just before he hung up, Sam said, with a tinge of concern in his voice, "Good luck, old buddy."

Thursday hesitated for a moment and then said, "Thanks, Sam."

Sam hung up the phone and then turned to Bartholomew.

"So," Sam asked, "what happened?"

"Well," said the frog, "when I left, I headed straight towards the villa of one of Colombia's biggest drug lords, Rafael Pelaez."

"Who?" I asked.

"Rafael Pelaez," Bartholomew answered, "He's this fat guy who's around 50. He's also a really big time criminal. He's worth billions of dollars and he lives in this house on the outskirts of Medellin. The place is practically sealed tight. It's got guards, and cameras, and machine gun posts and all that kind of stuff. Despite all the security, Rafael's always smiling and acting happy. He never gives away what he's really feeling. He just smiles and laughs and seems like a perfectly nice guy."

"But he isn't?" I guessed.

"Nope," Bartholomew said. "It's just a cover. He seems nice, but he's really a criminal mastermind. He loves money. But he loves something else even more. Power." Bartholomew continued, "When I hopped to Rafael's house, I landed on the perfect spot. I was on this pedestal on the balcony and I looked like a very realistic frog ornament. From where I was sitting I could see the Columbian mountains, but not Medellin itself. In Rafael's business there's a rule: if you can see somebody, chances are they can see you. For a man in Rafael's business, that's not an acceptable risk."

"What could you see?" I asked.

Bartholomew continued, "The pedestal had a great view of Rafael's driveway. When I hopped there, it had a view of Rafael himself. As I watched, I noticed two beautiful cars pull up, each accompanied by a huge number of motorcycles. Rafael was there, walking towards the cars, looking very welcoming. He seemed about ready to give the people in the cars a set of huge hugs. That was how he always acted. The thing was, I didn't expect him to be quite so welcoming to the people who were actually in the cars."

"Who were the people in the cars?" I asked.

"Jose Moreno and Alvaro Agudelo, Colombia's two *other* major drug lords. Being Columbian drug lords, they are also very dangerous people.

"Jose Moreno, the head of the Cali drug cartel, is a slight guy. He's also very young. He's 22 years old and one of the coolest guys you can imagine. He commands an army of thousands. His life is constantly in danger, but he never seems the least bit flustered, or friendly, or angry or sad. He's just smooth and certain of everything. They say that this guy never loves and never hates. He's just a machine, and a dangerous one at that."

"What about Alvaro?" I asked.

"Alvaro Agudelo is completely different. He's old for his business – over 60. But that's not the only way he's different from Jose. While

114

José and Rafael perfectly control their emotions, Alvaro has absolutely no control over his. Alvaro's this incredibly nervous guy. His hands shake when he talks, and he basically runs from personal confrontation. The amazing thing is that his obvious fear hasn't hurt his career. If anything, it's helped it. Alvaro's paranoia is so well-tuned that very few people can get close enough to challenge him. He might look scared, but that doesn't mean he's actually weak.

"I watched the three drug lords greet each other. José cooly shook Rafael's hand. But Alvaro didn't step away from the protection of his own bodyguards. Instead, he called Rafael over and shook his hand on his own territory – so to speak. Rafael was smiling at him. For a moment, Rafael actually seemed like a nice guy.

"I was very curious, but I was also a bit scared. I mean, these three men hated each other. They'd never even met each other before. As I watched them say hello to each other, I could only imagine one reason they'd gotten together – Grobar the Goat."

"How'd you figure out they were going to meet Grobar?" I asked.

"Patience," said Bartholomew. "I'm getting there. By the time the three men, and their bodyguards had made their way to Rafael's office, I was already there – waiting and watching. This time, I was sitting on the bookshelf. As I expected, drinks were not served. These men don't trust each other enough to drink together. And sure enough, as I watched, these three incredibly dangerous people suddenly stopped pretending to be friendly.

"'My friends,' said Rafael, flashing a crocodile smile, 'welcome. I have called each of you here for a meeting of the greatest importance. Between the three of us, we control almost the entire Colombian drug trade. Certainly the rebels and the paramilitary groups seem to have their own significant shares in the business, but, as all three of us know, those two groups pay us handsomely to actually distribute their products. Because of our dominance, none of us can expand in this business without taking a part of it away from the others. Where one of us succeeds, another must fail. I've called this meeting because I have discovered a route out of our deadly competition.'

"Alvaro, gray and frazzled, was eyeing Rafael nervously. His bodyguards were standing very close to him. Rafael's talk of cooperation clearly frightened him. Jose, on the other hand, didn't betray a thing. He was calmly resting his chin in his palm. But I knew he was considering Rafael's words very carefully.

"Rafael smiled, 'Yesterday, a young woman by the name of Marcella Parra paid me a visit.'

"When Rafael said that name, a shock went through the room."

"Who's Marcella Parra?" I asked.

"Marcella Parra is very interesting," Bartholomew said, "She's served as the go-between for the three men for a long time. She carries both threats and promises. She's a small, tightly built woman who is completely fearless. Marcella is the only person I've ever seen who can't be frightened. All three of the drug lords have tried to scare her into submission. And all three have failed. That's the reason Marcella is the only person they all trust completely. It's just how Marcella likes it."

"How do you know this stuff?" I asked.

"Eddy," said Bartholomew, "your dad told me that if I wanted to be good at this business then I needed to know everything I could about important people. Marcella is one of those people."

"Okay," I said, still uncertain how he knew so much about her.

"Alvaro is another one of those people," continued Bartholomew. "He's always been suspicious. Which is why I wasn't surprised when he asked, cautiously, 'Marcella Parra, are you sure?'

"'Yes,' said Rafael, still smiling. 'I can have her tell the rest of the story if you would prefer.'

"'Yes, I would prefer that,' said Alvaro.

"I knew that José also preferred to hear the story from Marcella. Of course, he wouldn't say so. He didn't want to give away any uncertainty. If you're a drug lord at the age of 22, you can't afford to seem the least bit weak.

"'Fine,' said Rafael. He lifted one of his plump little hands and then, as if on cue, Marcella Parra stepped into the room. Marcella walks with overwhelming power and self-assurance. She's not pretty; she doesn't try to make herself look pretty, but everybody's always looking at her. Most people simply fear her. But the three drug lords, who love power so much, completely adore her.

"Standing near a wall, Marcella began to speak, 'My dear friends,' her voice dripped with irony, 'I did come to Rafael Pelaez yesterday. I came bearing a message from a man named Grobar. This man, Grobar, has created a drug that grants him control over the minds of men. I have seen it in action, and it is powerful. He asked that I visit you and present you with a proposal.'"

"A man?" I interrupted. "Isn't he a goat?"

"He is a goat," said Bartholomew, "but he seems to have some local guy who stands in for him when talking to humans."

"Okay," I said.

Bartholomew continued, "All three drug lords leaned forward to listen to what Marcella had to say, 'This drug of Grobar's requires caffeine as a catalyst. Grobar is interested in modifying the coffee shipped from Colombia and Brazil to the rest of the world. He wants to add his drug to the beans. In return, he is willing to share the power he gains. I have seen the drug in action. With our help, this man Grobar can become quite powerful – and we can share in the spoils of his victories.'

"If the story had come from anyone but Marcella, the drug lords would have ignored it. But Marcella they trusted completely. While none of them said it, I knew all three were already planning to get the upper hand. All three planned to help this character Grobar and then to somehow force him to do their bidding. I know this because these aren't the kind of people who are interested in sharing power, not with each other, and not with anybody else. Grobar's offer already had them hooked.

"Jose might have been the youngest of the drug lords, but he was the first to speak. With his cold and precise voice he asked, 'Marcella, how can we contact this man Grobar?'

"Marcella answered, 'He would like to have a meeting at his facility. I'm afraid I don't know the exact location. Naturally, he is quite careful. But I do know how we can find it. It is along the 45th parallel. Grobar has suggested that we fly to Tripoli and then he will tell us what country he is in. Of course, there are shorter ways to go, but Libya is one of the few countries that will allow us to land. While we are flying along the 45th parallel, over the country he tells us to go to when we land in Tripoli, he will signal to us when we have reached his facilities.'

"Alvaro, his hands twitching, asked, 'Can we trust him enough to visit him on his terms?'

"This time, it was Rafael, chuckling, who answered, 'Yes, my dear friend, Alvaro Agudelo. He needs *our* help to carry out his plan. It would not be in his interest to harm us.'

"A few moments passed, each man considering the possibilities. Again José was the first to speak. Coolly, he said only three words, 'We should go.'

"'Yes,' said Rafael, smiling broadly. 'We should.'

"As always, cautious Alvaro was the last to speak. He pulled out a cigarette, fidgeted with it briefly and then finally agreed. 'I will go as well.' Despite his fear, he wasn't going to miss out on this opportunity.

"There was one more matter to attend to, how to get there. Rafael spoke up, 'My jet is waiting outside. I suggest we fly to Tripoli immediately!'

"'No,' said Alvaro. 'You might have some trick up your sleeve. Let us roll a die to determine whose plane we should take.' Alvaro handed Marcella his famous six-sided die."

"A famous six-sided die?" I asked.

"Exactly," said Bartholomew, "Alvaro always carries it. He has for years and years. It is a perfectly weighted die. He thinks that the element of chance will reduce the risks of his occupation. He has lived to 60, in an incredibly dangerous industry, so perhaps his theory had some weight. 'Marcella,' Alvaro continued, 'would you be so kind as to pick the numbers?'

"Marcella spoke, 'One or two, we take Alvaro's plane. Three or four, we take Rafael's plane. Five or six, we take Jose's plane. Agreed?' All three men agreed.

"Marcella rolled the die, and it was decided. With a phone call, Jose's Learjet was on its way. He announced that it would arrive in just under 25 minutes.

"That done, I came back here to tell Sam what was up."

"If Grobar and the drug lords hook up," I said, very seriously, "we're really going to be in trouble."

Bartholomew smiled thinly (especially thinly as he was a frog) and said, "Yes, Eddy, if Grobar and the drug lords hook up, we will certainly be in trouble."

(NARRATOR)

A Long Way from Lakedale

It didn't take long for Thursday to put two and two together. Grobar was in Mongolia – that he figured out from the language spoken at the factory. And Sam had told him that Grobar's headquarters were located on the 45th parallel. Using that information, he knew pretty much where he had to go. Before he got too far though, he radioed a quick message to PENGUIN HQ.

START TRANSMISSION
ASSAULT SUCCESSFUL
FACTORY SABOTAGED
INTEL SUGGESTS POSSIBLE HQ LOCATION IN MON-
GOLIA
SOURCE: GROBAR ON 45th PARALLEL
FLYING TO 45TH PARALLEL IN MONGOLIA NOW
END TRANSMISSION

The P-480 is a wonderful machine. It is fast, nimble and small. The P-480 could, at top speed, get to Mongolia in about 10 hours. The only problem is that going at top speed consumes a lot of fuel. For a long flight, like the flight to Mongolia, it just wasn't possible to fly at full speed the whole way. The P-480 would run out of fuel before it got very far. Instead, Thursday would have to fly at a slower speed – the same speed as a normal airplane. The P-480, for the bulk of its trip, would be no faster than the drug lord's plane.

If Thursday was going to beat the drug lords to Mongolia, he had to use any advantage he had. Luckily, he had two advantages. First, he could fly at full speed to the first refueling stop, just off San Francisco Bay. By doing so, he'd gain about 30 minutes on the drug lords. Second, he didn't have to fly as far as they did. Medellin was several hundred nautical miles further away from Mongolia than Lakedale was. All in all, by flying all night and refueling at PENGUIN's undersea refueling depots, he would get to Mongolia about an hour and a half ahead of the drug lords – even if they stopped to refuel in Tripoli. Of course, because the drug lords would take off in a half an hour, Thursday would actually get to his destination almost two hours ahead of them.

Knowing this, Thursday took off immediately. Two hours, in a trip that long, didn't leave a lot of breathing room. He couldn't afford to be late.

As he flew, Thursday wondered about 'The Source.' How was it possible that one person could learn so much?

Bartholomew, 'The Source,' knew far more than Thursday guessed. He knew how dangerous the drug lords and Grobar really were – and he knew just how much more dangerous they'd be if they teamed up. He knew that they had to be stopped. As Thursday and the drug lords raced to Grobar's headquarters, Bartholomew kept a close eye on both of them.

After a few hours at Sam's, listening to Bartholomew's reports, Eddy went home to sleep. He came back early the next morning, having somehow slipped in and out of the house without his mom noticing.

That entire day, Sam and Eddy waited for Barthlomew's regular reports. They heard him describe Thursday refueling in the Pacific Ocean. They listened as he described the dangerous mood on board the drug lord's jet. He even told them about Tripoli, the Libyan capital where the drug lords refueled their airplane. He also told them about the man who walked out of the airport terminal and announced that Mongolia was to be their destination.

The race was on, and Bartholomew was providing the play-by-play.

Either Thursday would get to Mongolia and stop Grobar, or the drug lords would join forces with the goat and take over the world.

(NARRATOR)

Global Emergency

Thursday (with Bartholomew looking over his shoulder) reached the eastern borders of Mongolia almost 20 hours after he left Lakedale. It was early in the morning Mongolian time. The flight had been very long and Thursday was exhausted. His penguin-sized belly also hurt a bit. He'd eaten quite a few ice creams on the way. While he wished he could take a nap, he knew that he couldn't. There wasn't much time to spare. The drug lords were only a few hours away.

The first place Thursday flew over was a town called Sainshand. He decided not to stop. After all, why would Grobar set up his base in a town? He had decided to build in one of the world's most empty countries, Mongolia. Building in a town just didn't make sense.

Bartholomew concurred.

Thursday headed further into Mongolia, flying directly over the Gobi Desert. The Gobi Desert is this famous featureless expanse covered with very short grass. It kind of resembles a giant hairy pancake with a buzz cut. Thursday's eyes were on the landscape, and on the instruments. He figured that in such terrain, Grobar's lair would stick right out.

He was correct, in a way.

About 200 miles into the desert, after passing numerous nomadic Mongolian dwellings (called Gers), Thursday's metal detector suddenly went wild. He looked out the window (so did Bartholomew), but they didn't see anything unusual. He was about to radio his position in to PENGUIN HQ when everything in the P-480 shut down. The whole thing just turned off. The instrument panel went completely blank, the engines stopped, and the little plane began to fall out of the sky. Thursday had no idea what was happening. But he wasn't the kind of fellow to panic. As the P-480 dropped out of the sky, Thursday manually activated the emergency parachute. With the parachute deployed, the P-480, Thursday, and Bartholomew floated gently to the ground. As they touched down, Thursday eyed his surroundings carefully.

There wasn't much to see.

After he hopped out behind Thursday, Bartholomew bit off the top of a piece of grass. He didn't do it because he was hungry. He did it in order to mark the desert. The mark didn't have to be big, it just had to be something he could superhop to.

As Bartholomew and Thursday looked around, each could see that the ground was flat in every direction. Every direction that is, but one. Something was sticking out of the desert. Thursday walked straight towards it. It looked very much like a phone box, except that it was painted to look like the desert. Actually, only the bottom half was painted like the desert grass. The top half was painted to look like the sky. The top was also painted like grass. He guessed, correctly, that the paint job was meant for humans. If you were a normal human height, you'd never notice it. Below the horizon it would be painted like grass, above the horizon it would look like the sky. And if you happened to be flying over, it would look grass too. It would be invisible. The thing was, Thursday wasn't quite as tall as a normal human. He was a foot tall. When he looked at the box, he saw this stretch of desert sticking much further out of the desert than everything around it. It looked pretty weird. So, he went to check it out.

The funny looking box was the same height as a phone box, but it had a bigger base. The walls were opaque; Thursday couldn't see inside. There was a button on it. It looked a lot like a doorbell. There was also something that looked a lot like a hand recognition system – except it was hoof shaped.

An idiot could have figured out that this was the entrance to Grobar's lair. Thursday wasn't an idiot, but that didn't stop him from figuring it out.

The problem was, Thursday knew that if he rang the doorbell, he would very soon be either a captive penguin or a dead penguin. If he didn't ring the doorbell, he would probably die of thirst. Either that, or the drug lords would arrive and deal with him in an even less pleasant way.

Thursday pondered his predicament.

And then, the answer to his troubles suddenly came to him.

Have you ever heard the phrase, 'Fish gotta swim and goats gotta breathe'? Well, Thursday hadn't either, but it was the clue he needed. If Grobar was living under this phone box, then he had to have some way of getting air. In short, there had to be an air vent.

Thursday walked around until he found it. It was 50 feet away and covered by a metal grate painted to look like the terrain around it. It was small, too small for most secret agents. But Thursday was only a foot-tall. Even suitcases don't make him feel claustrophobic. The vent wouldn't be a challenge.

Thursday attached his grappling arms and then quickly disman-tled the grate. He tied a standard PENGUIN-issue retracting rope to it, and then lowered himself into the hole.

Extending the rope, Thursday worked his way down. The vent wasn't one of those polished jobs you see in the movies. There were no metal walls. This vent was really just a hole in the ground – a narrow hole that went straight down. The only improvements were touches of mortar and of gravel that had been jammed into the walls to keep them from falling in. Somebody didn't care too much about presentation.

Thursday went about 50 feet before he encountered another air vent, this one going sideways, not straight down. He swung himself into it, releasing the retracting rope at just the right time. If you'll forgive the cliché, there was a dim light at the end of the tunnel – beneath it was another grate, which Thursday quickly pulled off.

Sticking his head through the hole, Thursday found himself in a janitor's closet. He knew it was a janitor's closet because no matter where you go, they always look the same.

Thursday was inside Grobar's headquarters.

The PENGUIN agent jumped into the room and quietly opened the closet door. Bartholomew hopped in right behind him. There was a hallway in front of them. It had the same rocky walls the vent had had, except that these walls were reinforced by concrete ribs.

The lighting was very dim.

There were six doors leading off the hallway. All six had buttons next to them. Five of the doors were labeled. Had Thursday been feeling particularly adventuresome, he would have hit the button on the unlabeled door. But he went for a 'safer' choice. He hit the button on a door marked "Grobar."

Moments later, the door slid open. It was an elevator door. It opened with a ding. As soon as Thursday looked inside the elevator, he realized that it wasn't empty. And the character in the elevator wasn't some dorky looking elevator operator. Actually, it might have been an elevator operator. But it wasn't dorky looking, or at least you wouldn't say so to its face. What it was, was one mean-looking robot. And a very tall one.

As Thursday's eyes slowly made their way up the robot's body, the robot's eyes slowly made their way down to Thursday (he *was* really short).

When the robot finally saw him, it pulled out a club.

Thursday turned to run. His blow gun wouldn't do anything to this robot. He didn't get very far.

With a thud, the robot brought its club down on Thursday's head.

The little penguin collapsed. He didn't look dead, but he was certainly down for the count.

Bartholomew had been watching everything. But he couldn't do a thing against the robot.

In a panic, he superhopped back to Eddy and Sam.

(SHORT EDDY)

Hopping Mad

"I'M NOT GOING TO LET IT HAPPEN AGAIN!"

Bartholomew had suddenly appeared on the table in Sam's warehouse. He scared me, and he scared Sam. But Sam calmed down quickly, and asked, in a confused voice, "Not let *what* happen again?"

"I'm not going to let another one of my friends get killed!" responded Bartholomew, angrily.

"What's wrong with Thursday?" asked Sam, suddenly very worried.

"One of Grobar's robots got him, hit him right on the head. I think he's okay, but I can't tell. What I can tell you is that that goat is going down." Bartholomew was gritting his non-teeth.

"Calm down, we've got to think about what to do," said Sam, his deep and methodical voice making me feel pretty laid back. He wasn't laid back, but that didn't stop him from having a tremendously calming influence.

Bartholomew didn't seem affected though. "There's no time for thinking. The drug lords are less than an hour and a half away. We've got to do something, NOW!"

"But what?" I asked.

"We've got to get somebody there, and fast, to save Thursday and kick that goat in his short furry tail."

128

"Who?" asked Sam, still trying to be calm.

"PENGUIN's Beijing agent," announced Bartholomew. "I'll go pay him a visit *right now*."

"NO!" shouted Sam.

"Why not?" asked Bartholomew, "and the clock is ticking." He didn't have much patience for Sam right then.

"Because," said Sam, "Thursday is the best PENGUIN has. If he couldn't do it, some agent from Beijing isn't going to do any better."

"Okay," said Bartholomew, "I'll get the Ferret Legion." He looked like he was ready to hop.

"NO!" shouted Sam.

"What now?" asked Bartholomew, getting a little annoyed.

"You and I both know they are completely tied up in the Gopher Wars. They can't possibly help. Plus, they can't get there fast enough."

"So who do you suggest?" asked Bartholomew, frustrated.

Sam just stood there, thinking.

Just as he was getting ready to nod his head in resignation (elephants take a long time to nod their heads), I had an idea. "What about the Gryffin?" I asked, holding my breath a bit because I wasn't sure my idea was any good.

"The Gryffin?" said Bartholomew. "Your dad just used it to get around. And as far as I know, PENGUIN agents can't ride in it. Plus, it's not a weapon. So," he barked, "How can it possibly help?"

He was in a positively horrible mood.

"How fast could my dad get around?" I asked.

"Real fast," said Bartholomew, "but who cares?"

"Because," I said, "I'll bet that *I* can use it. I can go to Mongolia and I can save Thursday and teach that goat a lesson."

"You?" said Bartholomew. He wasn't very convinced. Then he brightened up a bit, "Well," he said, "I guess if anybody has a chance, you do. Let's get to it!"

"NO!" shouted Sam, really insistent this time.

"What now?" asked Bartholomew.

"Are you going to risk Eddy to try to save Thursday?" He wasn't talking to me, we were still keeping our promise to Thursday.

Bartholomew just sat there, glumly, looking at Sam.

"Yes," *I* said to Bartholomew. "You're going to do exactly that."

"What is he talking about?" demanded Sam. "This isn't a game. Grobar and the drug lords are very dangerous people."

"Exactly," I said, addressing Bartholomew, "Thursday's not the only one at risk here. The whole world is. As you said, these guys are dangerous. That's exactly why something needs to be done. I have to give it a try."

"I won't let him go," said Sam. He made a move to the door, his massive frame very successfully blocking it.

The poor little frog hadn't had a chance to get a word in edgewise – and Sam and I weren't even talking to each other.

Finally, he spoke, "Sam, it's his risk and his choice. You and I also know that it's his destiny."

I had no idea what he meant about destiny, but I could understand the rest, so I interjected, "It is my risk and I want to go."

Reluctantly, Sam backed away from the door and headed to the phone.

He picked up the phone in his trunk. He then used his feet to dial a few numbers on a huge pad. A few seconds later he said, "Hello ... yes ... can you send a car to ACME Toe Jam and Toast? It is at 4800 NW Edison ... We're in a tremendous rush."

Bartholomew turned to me and said, "I'll see you back at your place. Tell the driver he's got a big tip coming if he gets you back home quickly." In a single leap, he disappeared. Two minutes later, a cab honked from outside the warehouse.

As Sam wished me good luck, I ran outside, hopped in the back seat of the cab, and seat belted myself in as the driver took off.

(SHORT EDDY)

The Gryffin

I got home really really really quickly. I mean, the cabbie just floored it. We flew along the freeway and got back to my house in 15 minutes flat, in record time. I know it was 15 minutes because I was timing it on my watch. When we were almost there, Bartholomew appeared in my shirt pocket and handed me a $100 bill. That's a lot of money. Almost enough for 200 candy bars. He told me not to ask for change. When the cab reached my house, I gave the driver the $100 bill and he gave me a 100-watt smile and we both came away with what we wanted.

That done, I dashed out of the cab and ran upstairs. I quickly activated the system that lets me into my room and then I headed straight for the Gryffin. Bartholomew was already there. "So," I asked him, "how do we use this thing?"

Bartholomew answered immediately, "I don't know."

He seemed annoyed. He was definitely impatient. He was hopping back and forth on my desk. It was quite disconcerting.

"STOP HOPPING!" I shouted.

He stopped. But now his eyes were blinking really rapidly.

"Can you tell me anything?" I asked.

He thought for a moment. "I know your dad used it, but I have no idea how he turned it on. I can't super-hop inside it, I've tried. I'll bet your dad left you some key to turn it on though. I mean, if he wanted you to use it, he had to give you some way to turn it on."

"My dad didn't leave me much," I said. "The only unusual things are the access system for my room and the Gryffin itself."

"Well," said Bartholomew, a little impatiently, "maybe that access system is it. Do whatever you do to get into your room with the Gryffin."

It was a good suggestion, so I followed it. I put my hand on the Gryffin, looked straight at it, and said, "My name is Edward."

Nothing happened.

Then, I had another idea. I ran outside my room, put my hand on the door handle, looked at it and said, "Turn on the Gryffin." Still, nothing happened.

I got back inside my room as fast as I could, then I said to Bartholomew, "No luck. Can you hop to where this key is located?"

Bartholomew didn't even bother replying. Instead, he just took a super-hop, disappeared and then reappeared right where he had started. He looked up, "There is a key, and it's in here. Please find it, while there is still time."

Where though?

Bartholomew asked, "Did your dad leave you anything besides the access system?"

I answered, "Well, he probably left me pretty much everything in this room. But there's a lot of stuff in here. I have no idea where it would be."

"Are there any unusual toys? Something other kids don't have?"

"Nope," I said, "nothing like that. My parents aren't really into toys."

"Hey!" I said, "Maybe, I should ask my mom if she knows if my dad left me anything special besides the entry system?"

"Good idea," said Bartholomew, trying to usher me out of the room with spastic movements of his little arms.

I ran out of my room, but before I could get downstairs, the frog suddenly appeared on the stairs in front of me. "Back upstairs!" he ordered.

So I turned around and ran back upstairs. I was very confused. When we got back into my room, Bartholomew said, "*You* have the key. You are carrying it with you. I super-hopped to the key again, after you left the room, and that is how I ended up on the staircase."

It was then that I remembered the photograph of my dad, the one I always carried around in my back pocket. I pulled it out, removed the waterproof wrapper and held it up. It didn't look like a key to me. But it did to Bartholomew. "Turn it over," he said. So I did. And there, written on the back of the photograph, was a word I had never noticed before – 'Arslan.'

"Say it," said Bartholomew.

So I did, and that was when things began to get really weird. When I said the word, 'Arslan,' the Gryffin floated off the table and then expanded in the middle of my room. The small sphere just became a bigger sphere – it was almost like pieces that had been inside the Gryffin had just popped out to form part of the bigger ball. It was pretty cool. Then another really cool thing happened, a hole just opened in the side of the Gryffin. It was a pretty big hole and it was very dark on the inside. "What do I do?" I asked.

Bartholomew didn't hesitate. "Get in," he said.

I wasn't exactly sure what I wanted to do. But Bartholomew didn't seem to think anything was weird. So I got in.

There was a seat inside, and it fit me perfectly. As soon as I hopped in, the door closed. It was pitch black inside. I was hoping Bartholomew hadn't given me some really bad advice. Then, slowly, as I watched, instruments began to appear. Even cooler, the front of the sphere became a window – like the kind a helicopter has. Through it, I could see my room, and I could see that I was floating above my bedroom floor.

I was still getting oriented, when I heard a soft voice, "What is our destination?" I remember thinking, 'Wow! The Gryffin talks!'

Where did I want to go? I didn't know exactly, but Bartholomew had been talking about the 45th parallel in Mongolia, so I said, "The 45th parallel in Mongolia."

Then the system said, "Target acceptable. However, your bedroom window would be damaged in transit."

Doh!

I suddenly realized we couldn't get through the window. With the Gryffin expanded, we just wouldn't fit. My mom would kill me if I smashed my way through my bedroom window so I said, trying to make it sound official, "Exit vehicle." Almost before I stopped talking, the side of the Gryffin opened and I stepped back out into my bedroom. Bartholomew was there. "What happened?" he asked, patiently. "Well," I said, "I can fly to Mongolia, but the Gryffin won't fit through the window so we'll have to carry it outside first."

"Okay," said Bartholomew. "I'm going to check on the drug lords while you carry it outside. I'll meet you on the front lawn before you leave."

"Fine," I said.

In an instant, Bartholomew disappeared.

I turned to the Gryffin and then, on an impulse, I said "Shrink." And it did. It became even smaller than usual. It became really really small. I mean, the thing suddenly fit in my pocket!

Whatever it was, the Gryffin was extremely cool.

I quickly ran downstairs. I thought about asking my mom for permission to go to Mongolia. But I knew what she'd say. She'd say, "Sure," without believing a word that I said. So I just ran outside without getting permission. Bartholomew was waiting for me, "The drug lords are almost in Mongolia. You better get going, and now!" I didn't bother answering him. Instead, I said 'Arslan' again and the Gryffin expanded. A hole appeared just like the last time. Just before I hopped in, Bartholomew said, "I can't get into that thing. I just can't hop into it. So I can't tell you when you get close to Grobar's facility. If you possibly can, you are going to have to find where the drug lord's plane lands. Just remember, they are going someplace on the 45th parallel in Mongolia."

"Okay," I answered. Then I hopped in and commanded the Gryffin, "Go to the 45 parallel in Mongolia."

I almost got sick when the Gryffin moved. I mean, I could see out the front window; I could even look down. That's what I was doing when the ground just dropped away. I mean, I didn't feel like I had moved or anything, but all of sudden the ground was very, very far away. I almost puked. It was pretty upsetting, to my stomach I mean. I kept going up, like one of those movies where they zoom in on a neighborhood from space, but this time it was backwards. We, the Gryffin and I, were hustling. And then, once we had gotten up real high – not quite in space, but it felt like we were close – the Gryffin just changed direction and headed straight for the ocean. Now, I don't live near the ocean, but because I was so high up, I could still see it stretching out ahead of me. It was hundreds of miles away – at least – but we got to it in like two minutes. As we flew over it, I could see ships beneath me. They were like tiny specks. I even saw Hawaii as we passed it. But we just kept going – keeping up our incredibly fast pace. I know it must have been around 30 minutes before we got to Mongolia, but it felt like two hours. I would have checked, but my watch seemed to have stopped working. It was just so cool. When we got to the border of Mongolia, at the 45th parallel, the Gryffin asked, again, "Where would you like to go?"

It was very early in the morning in Mongolia. As I looked around, I could see a tiny speck in the distance. It might have been an airplane. So I asked, "Can we zoom in on that speck?" What happened next was really weird; the speck started to grow. It wasn't like we were getting closer. Everything aside from the speck stayed right where it was. But a small part of the view screen was zooming in on the speck. It was like a magnifying glass or a telescope, except that nothing except the speck was getting magnified. As the speck grew larger and larger, taking up more of the screen, I could see that it was a jet airplane. And a nice one. And it was landing in the middle of this huge flat plain. So I said, "Fly there." The Gryffin shot forward again, heading straight for the airplane. It couldn't have taken more than a minute to get there. We arrived just as the airplane landed.

I decided to try something. I asked the Gryffin, "Scan the desert for a frog." I didn't know if anything would happen, but then the whole zooming in thing happened really quickly. It wasn't like the time when I zoomed up on the airplane. Nope, this time the magnified area was shifting all over my view of the desert. Then, suddenly, it stopped moving. There, super-zoomed in on, was Bartholomew. I instructed the Gryffin to land there, and it did. We were about 100 feet from the jet.

The hole on the Gryffin opened and I hopped out. "Shrink," I said. The Gryffin shrunk. I stuck the now tiny Gryffin in my pocket. As soon as the Gryffin was safely stashed away, I 'hit the deck,' lying down on the short grass of the Mongolia plain. Bartholomew was right next to me. I was very happy to be on the ground. Standing up on the plain would have made me a really obvious target. Laying down helped me hide. More importantly, it gave my sick stomach a chance to recover from the trip. I was laying there, watching, when I saw the drug lords and their posse walk into something that looked like a phone booth.

Bartholomew whispered in my ear, "You'd better get a move on, Grobar is getting close to sealing this deal!"

"I know," I said, a bit frustrated that he was pointing out the obvious. I knew I had to stop the meeting, but I didn't know what to do. I did know that I was running out of time, though. So, I got up and ran to where the phone box was. There was a button on it. I pushed the button, figuring it was probably a doorbell.

I was right.

A few moments after I hit the button, the phone box opened.

A very friendly-looking animal was inside.

As our eyes met, I realized that I was face-to-face with none other than Grobar the Goat.

(SHORT EDDY)

Face to Face

I was face to face with Grobar and I was pretty scared.

Grobar spoke first, "Who are you?"

I thought really quickly, so quickly that I'm still proud of myself. Putting on my best Latin American accent I said, "My name is Eduardo Pelaez, I am the son of Rafael Pelaez." I had no idea whether Rafael had a son, but I guessed, correctly, that Grobar didn't know either.

"What do you want?" asked Grobar.

"My father asked me to watch his back, now that I have made sure there is nothing out here, I am to meet him inside." My accent was really pretty good. Nonetheless, Grobar seemed a little unconvinced. I added a little sauce, "If you, little goat, don't lead me to my father, I will have you served for dinner. If you do, little goat, lead me to my father, then we can be friends. That would be best, would it not?"

I guess I had said something right, because Grobar said, "I'll be glad to be your friend, but don't threaten me. I don't like it when people say mean things." Grobar stood to the side and I stepped into the phone box, which turned out to be a really cool elevator. It only had two buttons. Grobar pressed the lower one and then we shot downwards. When the doors opened, I found myself looking down a dimly lit hallway. At the end of the hall, there was a robot who saluted when it saw us.

We didn't stay in the hallway for long. Instead, we turned to the first door on the left. Grobar hit a button and it opened. It was another elevator. I guess somebody liked elevators. Grobar gestured me in. Figuring I had no choice, I stepped inside – leaving Grobar behind. The doors closed, I moved, the doors opened, and I found myself in a dimly lit room. There was a table, some chairs, four dark and rocky walls and – as I expected – three drug lords. They (and their associates) were just as Bartholomew had described them.

Everybody in the room was holding a wine glass filled with a dark substance. There was one guy in the room who didn't fit with the rest. He was lighter skinned. It stuck out against the dark background of the room. I could immediately tell that he was a Mongolian. What I didn't know was that his name was Altan. He was talking as I came in, "... a toast to the success of our endeavor!" The drug lords raised their glasses. Then, they saw me.

When my supposed father, Rafael Pelaez asked, a smile on his face, "Who are you?" I knew the dominoes were about to fall.

"Don't drink the toast!" I shouted, thinking as quickly as I could. "Grobar's drugged the drinks!" It was about the only thing I could think to say. I was really running on some pretty empty batteries.

But do you know what? It worked. The room just exploded with activity. I ducked under the table when I saw two groups of robots come out of two side rooms. Hiding under the table, I heard an extremely loud burst of gunfire and lots of other noises as the drug lords battled with the robots. I peeked my head out when things had died down. Robot parts were everywhere. All the people were still standing. That left 3 drug lords, 9 bodyguards, 1 Marcella and 1 Mongolian man. It didn't take much to see who had won that fight.

As I came out from under the table, the falsely jovial Rafael Pelaez said, "Gracias, poco niño."

Turning to the Mongolian, Rafael said, "Grobar, at some point we are going to take the recipe from you. We'd like this to be nice, friendly and pleasant. It will be a lot easier if you just tell us the recipe for your mind control drug."

In case you missed it, a few things had just happened. First, Rafael had just called the Mongolian dude Grobar. Which meant Bartholomew was right. The real Grobar had tricked them into thinking he was human. Second, they asked the Mongolian dude for the recipe. Now, I guarantee you the Mongolian dude didn't know the recipe, he was just being controlled by Grobar's drug. And third, they threatened to torture him. Now, if Grobar was in control of this Mongolian guy, there was no way he'd talk. I knew they were barking up the wrong tree – but I wasn't about to tell them. The mind control drug in the hands of the drug lords would be just as bad as the mind control in the hands of Grobar – maybe worse. The only reason it might be better if the drug lords had the recipe was that they would try to kill each other to gain control over it.

Just as I guessed, the Mongolian said nothing. Not a word.

So José Moreno tried his hand at intimidation, "Grobar, we will start by pulling off your toenails. Then, we will pull off your toes. Then, we will pull off your feet. And so on and so forth until every part of you has been pulled off. Of course, if you tell us what we want to know, none of this need happen." He said all of this in a completely flat and emotionless voice. It was pretty scary.

But still, the Mongolian said absolutely nothing.

Then, still quivering from the recent battle, the twitchy Alvaro gave it his best shot. "Do you think you can scare us!" he shouted, shaking in fear and rage. "You can't. Speak up or it will be all over for you."

140

The Mongolian stood absolutely still and said absolutely nothing. It was pretty clear to me that Grobar didn't much care about this particular Mongolian.

Jose pulled out a pocket knife, walked up to the Mongolian, and stabbed him in the hand. The Mongolian didn't even blink. By then it was becoming pretty clear, even to Jose, that there was no way he was going to talk. So José barked, "Bodyguards! All of you, search this place."

The bodyguards immediately scattered, scarcely giving Alvaro the chance to protest his sudden lack of protection. Marcella encouraged the drug lords to take seats at the table I had been hiding beneath. It was only a matter of a few minutes before the first bodyguard returned, popping out the elevator I had come down in. He had a goat in one hand and a Overnight Express package in his other hand. "Boss," he said to Jose, "I found this goat chewing on this package."

Jose grabbed the package and calmly opened it. It contained a single, empty, vial. It was labeled, "Mind Drug, Batch #1." There were no ingredients, nothing. I was pretty happy about that until José turned the package over and carefully read the return address:

"KIDD PHARMACEUTICALS
280 NW FREMONT
LAKEDALE, USA"

Just like that, the drug lords knew where Grobar's factory was! With a wave of his fingers, José had his bodyguards tie me up. He also tied up the Mongolian and the real Grobar. Last but not least, another one of the bodyguards returned holding Thursday in his hand. Thursday was still knocked out cold. The bodyguard tied Thursday up too. As he did so, he wondered aloud, "What is a Penguin doing in the middle of the Gobi Desert?"

The drug lords had us all – all but Bartholomew, who wasn't so easy to catch.

Pulling out a radio phone, José spoke clearly and carefully, "Operatives 3C, 4D and 7Q, converge on KIDD PHARMACEUTI-CALS, 280 NW FREMONT, Lakedale, USA. Retrieve all laboratory notes and plans." Just like that, the drug lords had operatives racing to steal Grobar's recipe.

Then, he turned to us. The other two drug lords watched carefully as José spoke, "I'm sorry, I can't allow you to leave this place."

We all nodded our heads dumbly. I couldn't believe it. A Colombian drug lord was about to execute me in the middle of Mongolia and my mom would probably never figure out where I went and she'd be very worried. When I thought about it, I realized she'd be worried for a pretty good reason. At that moment, I wished I'd asked her for her permission – at least she'd know where I'd gone.

But just then, something else happened.

Remember Marcella?

Well, she snapped her fingers and in a millisecond all 9 body-guards had converged on the drug lords. Moments later, they too were lined up against the wall. They were very very very confused and that is an understatement. Even Jose, the cool hand of the group, looked a bit upset. Marcella eyed the three of them and said, carefully, "I've been manipulating all of you for years. You trusted me because I wasn't scared of you. Because of that, each of you figured that I would never side with one of the other two. And you were right, I never did. But none of you considered that I might have my own agenda."

"What are you talking about!" demanded Rafael.

"Well," said Marcella, "I've befriended all your bodyguards. They know each other better than you know them and I know your organizations inside and out. The time has come for a unified Colombian drug cartel – built off of the stupidity of you three blind mice."

142

The bodyguard who brought in Grobar and the package said, "Yeah, that's right, us bodyguards are sick of fighting each other. We figured it would be a lot better if we all had the same boss."

Marcella looked at him with mild annoyance; he was in the middle of her groove.

Alvaro sputtered, "A-a-are you going to kill us?"

"Yes," said Marcella, jubilantly, "it's my turn, boys."

Alvaro's face dropped. I could see José was already working on the ropes that restrained him.

Then Marcella turned to the bodyguards. With another snap of her fingers they pulled out their weapons. Marcella started counting, "Five."

Alvaro was sweating buckets.

"Four."

Rafael started praying under his breath.

"Three."

Grobar lowered his head. Thursday was still unconscious.

"Two."

The Mongolian did nothing.

"One."

I thought about my mom.

And then, right before Marcella hit "Zero," the most amazing thing happened.

(SHORT EDDY)

Something Amazing

I said something amazing happened? Well, actually, two things happened. First, all the bodyguard's pistols just flew out of their hands and stuck to the ceiling. Actually, everything metal did that – even the table. It was like a huge magnet had been turned on. Second, 10 penguins – wearing black commando outfits complete with ski masks – charged into the room from the elevator. Each had a blow gun. I would have laughed at the sight of the waddling commandos, but they were saving my life.

Seconds later, it was all over. Nobody even had time to be surprised. After I blinked, every one of the drug lords and bodyguards, even Marcella, Grobar and the Mongolian, had collapsed on the floor. Thursday told me later that they'd all been hit with Forget-Me darts.

Once the action was over, a single human walked into the room. That human was covered head to toe in a black outfit, which also included a ski mask. A penguin, who I would later come to know as CSO July, spoke up, "Commander-in-Chief, the targets have been neutralized."

With a click of the Commander's fingers, the penguins undid my bonds. A penguin-sized stretcher appeared and Thursday was loaded onto it. Before carrying him away, the penguin paramedics did a quick check on him and then confirmed to the Commander that he would be all right. Then, a pair of four-legged leg-irons appeared. They were strapped onto Grobar. He was still sleeping. One of the penguins told me that he'd be "imprisoned in Antarctica."

With another motion, all the penguins – and the commander and I – walked briskly out of the room. We left the drug lords and their retinue sleeping where they were. The Forget-Me darts had wiped out their short-term memory. They would have no idea how they got to where they were, and, more importantly, they wouldn't remember anything about PENGUIN commandos. Instead, they would eventually wake up, find their bearings, and fly home (of course the Mongolian wouldn't have to fly anywhere to get home). None of them would know how they ended up in a secret facility under the Gobi desert, though they might try to figure it out – which is why they would have to be monitored.

Quickly, we headed up the stairs and out into the sunlight. I felt Bartholomew super-hop into my pants pocket, sharing the space with the shrunken Gryffin.

Outside, parked in the middle of the desert, was a full-size cargo plane. It was actually a 737 that'd been converted and painted black and white just like a penguin. All around the plane there were lots of the personal fighter jets of the sort I'd seen in Thursday's office. The drug lord's Learjet was there too, but everybody just seemed to ignore it. Instead, most of the penguins hopped into their personal fighter jets and took to the air.

Not everybody got into a personal jet though. CSO July, the Commander-in-Chief and a couple of extra penguins climbed into the 737. I climbed in too. There were a few military style seats up near the front of the plane, and a couple of penguins were at the controls. The rest of the plane seemed to be filled with all sorts of equipment. I guessed that this was PENGUIN's version of a SWAT van.

145

The doors closed, we strapped ourselves in and then, with a PENGUIN fighter escort, the plane took off.

It was then, once we were off the ground, that I turned to the Commander and said, quite seriously, "Thank you very much, sir, for saving our lives."

The Commander turned to me and peeled off the ski mask.

I almost passed out when I saw the face beneath the mask. Under the ski mask, there was a woman. And that woman was none other than my mom.

Yes, you heard me right. My mom.

I just stared at her, completely confused. What was SHE doing here? What about all those notes? Had she just been pretending not to believe me?

"Eddy, I'm really sorry it took so long to get here. We didn't know exactly where Grobar was until José Moreno sent that radio message out. I was worried about you; I figured you'd probably get here somehow."

"Mom," I asked, still shocked, "who are you?"

"I'm your mom," she answered, calmly, "But I am also the Commander-in-Chief of PENGUIN, the agency Thursday works for."

"Why didn't you tell me?" I asked.

"Because I didn't want to worry you. You'd already lost your dad, I didn't want you to be scared you'd lose me too. I even left that one notebook lying around just to make sure you didn't guess."

It was beginning to sink in that she was for real. "So why'd you let me get involved with Thursday?"

She took a big breath and then answered, slowly, "Eddy. I love you very much. So much I'm sometimes scared I don't let you do the things you need to do. I knew you could help with the case, so I made a decision. I let you get involved, and I even helped some. Why do you think I drove you to get your bike? I did it because I thought it would be good for you. I also did it because I knew it would be good

146

for the world. But I was still worried sick. It was one of the hardest things I've ever done. I'm really proud you did such a good job." Her eyes had this kinda bittersweet look, so I reached over and gave her a big hug. She returned the favor and then I knew; she really was my mom – and she really was the Commander-in-Chief of the world's premier spy agency.

CSO July interrupted our hug. "I'm sorry, sir, we aren't in the clear yet. José Moreno sent that message. The drug lords will get their hands on that recipe very soon if we don't somehow stop them first. The problem is that all the PENGUIN agents are here and we can't possibly get to Lakedale before the bad guys."

"I could fly the Gryffin there," I offered.

"No good," said July, "Even you couldn't get there in time."

I could feel Bartholomew disappear from my pocket, but I had no idea what he was up to. "It's the best we can do," I said. "I might be able to stop them on the way out."

July and I looked to the Commander-in-Chief, my mom, and she nodded her head.

With that, I pulled the Gryffin out of my pocket and said the code word that expanded it. Just before I got in, my mom spoke up. "Eddy, I love you. Fly carefully."

"Okay mom," I said, although I wasn't that worried. With that I climbed in and watched as the hole closed behind me. A penguin helpfully opened the door of the plane. We were still at a low altitude, so everything didn't get sucked out. Then, with a word to the Gryffin, I flew straight into the open sky.

I'd be in Lakedale in about 30 minutes. I hoped that would be fast enough.

(NARRATOR)

Elephant Attack

Bartholomew knew a few things about drug lords. One of them was that it wasn't going to take 30 minutes for operatives 3C, 4D and 7Q (the drug lord's operatives) to take over Grobar's factory. Something else had to be done, and quickly.

As Eddy talked to his mom, Bartholomew decided he had to go see Sam. With a single super-hop, he was on his favorite table at ACME Toe Jam and Toast – Sam the Elephant's home.

"Sam!" shouted Bartholomew, looking around for Sam. Sam had been waiting for Bartholomew too, but he was behind him.

"Yup?" said Sam.

"We've got an emergency, Sam."

"Did something happen to Eddy?" asked Sam, really worried.

"No, no, Eddy's fine. In fact, he did great and helped stop Grobar cold. Thursday's fine too. He did a great job."

"So what's wrong?" asked Sam, patiently.

"The problem is, well – it's the drug lords. They've got three guys heading over to Grobar's factory to get their hands on Grobar's secret recipe."

"How soon will Eddy get here?" asked Sam, his head tipped to the side.

"It'll take Eddy a half hour to get here, but if the drug lords have somebody in town, they'll get to the factory a lot faster than that."

"Uh oh," said Sam, "we're the only ones in Lakedale, aren't we?"

"Yup," said Bartholomew.

"So," said Sam, "I guess that it's up to us to do something about that factory."

"The question," said Bartholomew, "is what to do?"

Sam rested his giant head on his giant trunk (which was resting on the table), and began to think.

"Well," said Bartholomew, "I can hop to where the recipe and the laboratory notes are, but I can't possibly destroy them. There are too many notes, and I'm just too small."

"Okay," said Sam, done thinking, "I know what I've got to do."

"What's that?" asked Bartholomew.

"I've got to get over there and destroy the recipe myself," announced Sam, determination written all over his massive face. "I'm certainly not too small."

"How are you going to fit in the doors?" asked Bartholomew.

"I'm not," said Sam.

"Then how are you going to get the recipe?" asked Bartholomew.

With a smile Sam announced, "I guess I'll have to make my own door."

A minute later, Sam, the always reclusive elephant, was galloping down the middle of NW Edison. Nearby buildings shook, car alarms went off, and pedestrians scrambled in terror.

Sam was on the move.

Perched on the very top of his head, surveying the entire terrain, was none other than Bartholomew the Frog with Precision Hopping Ability.

Two-hundred eighty NW Fremont, the home of Kidd Pharmaceuticals, was only 10 blocks away.

When Sam and Bartholomew got there, the drug lord's operatives were just arriving. Drug operatives, 3C, 4D and 7Q were not slouches. They were the best of the best – and they worked for the worst of the worst. They were just getting their tools out of the trunk of their car and they were about to become very, very dangerous.

Sam didn't even stop to assess the situation.

Without a second thought, Sam stomped on the trunk of their car – and kept on going.

The operatives weren't finished yet. They preferred to work with the stuff that'd been in the trunk, but they didn't need to. They still had their guns and they still had a fine selection of grenades. Within seconds, they'd drawn their weapons and rushed the loading dock of Kidd Pharmaceuticals. They weren't interested in Sam – their goal was the recipe and as far as they knew Sam was just a rogue elephant.

When Grobar got knocked unconscious, his operatives were temporarily freed. That included his operatives in the factory in Lakedale, USA. Thankfully for Grobar at least, they could see the signs on the walls. And posted on the walls, in Mongolian, were signs that read:

"Protect this building – there are great financial rewards if you do. Follow lit arrows on the floor to the armory."

After looking out the windows and being very, very confused, they decided that they'd better follow the instructions. So they went to the armory, just as the drug lord's operatives were arriving. Another sign told them to press a button, so they did. And then the normal looking commercial building in Northwest Lakedale was transformed. Bulletproof shutters dropped over all the windows and doors, including the loading docks. There was only one exception. A small steel door – securely locked from the inside, on the street side of the factory. The signs in the armory told them to defend it.

Operatives 3C, 4D and 7Q turned towards that room. One tossed a grenade that blew the door open like it was made of confetti. All three of them then rushed the door, weapons at the ready. Grobar's operatives were waiting in fortified positions on the other side.

Sam wasn't involved in that fight. As planned, Sam didn't head for the loading dock, or the windows or even that little steel door where all the fighting was taking place.

Nope, he headed right for the side of the building. Bartholomew was crouched behind his ears as he made his final assault.

With an earth-shattering boom, Sam met the building and the building met Sam. Although both shuddered, neither gave way. Sam hadn't succeeded in making his own door.

So, he backed up and tried again.

This time, the building gave more than he did – but there was still no door.

In that fortified hallway, Grobar's operatives watched as the walls swayed around them. They had no idea what was going on, but they weren't about to surrender.

3C and 4D each tossed smoke grenades into the corridor. Moments later, Grobar's operatives were completely blinded. They shot into the hallway, trying to stop the impending assault through guesswork. Then 7Q tossed in a stun grenade. Everybody in that hallway was disoriented. That was enough for 3C, 4D and 7Q to rush in.

It was just then that Sam gave his third and final push.

He still didn't make his own door. Instead, with a huge groan from the structural steel, the low slung building bent completely sideways. As Sam kept pushing, the entire thing gave way. Just like that, everybody in the hallway was buried under the rubble. They weren't badly hurt, but they were certainly going to be out of action for a bit.

With the entire facility now flattened, Sam peeked over the ruins and immediately identified the laboratory.

He stampeded over to it, stomping over desks, machine tools and lots of other kinds of stuff. The lab was filled with beakers, computers and stacks of handwritten notes. With a sweep of his trunk, Sam sent the beakers flying. He then turned on the notes.

Bartholomew was doing his part too. He super hopped to the computers and then super hopped from key to key – very, very quickly entering the commands needed to completely clear their hard disks.

There was an industrial-sized blender in the lab.

There were also some kiwis.

Sam took all the notes and a bunch of the kiwis and threw them in the blender.

He ran the blender at its highest speed for 30 seconds. Then he turned it off, picked it up, and drank down the kiwi-flavored notes.

Just like that, everything important had been destroyed.

Sam was about to bound off, leaving the drug lords and Grobar's operatives to their fates.

But before he could escape, the police arrived.

(SHORT EDDY)

One Week Later

I have never seen such a sad elephant. I mean the big guy, Sam, was really down. He was laying on the ground, his trunk was stretched out in front of him, his legs were sprawled in every direction, and he was crying. He was really, really unhappy.

Why?

Because he was in the Lakedale Zoo – his least favorite place in the entire world.

When I first showed up, he hadn't even notice me.

In case you don't remember, Sam escaped from the Zoo when he was little (or as little as elephants get). He left behind his mom and his dad and he never saw them again – ever. All just to escape the Zoo. Some elephants like the zoo because they like the attention, but Sam wasn't one of them. Sam just wanted to wilt away – he didn't want to be a celebrity and he didn't want to be stuck behind bars.

Even when I walked right up to the bars on his pen, Sam still didn't notice me.

"Hey, Sam!" I whispered. Thursday had released me from my promise, so I could talk to him all I wanted.

Sam's head popped up, slowly. "Hey, Eddy," he said, in an incredibly depressed voice.

"I've brought you some nuts," I said.

"Okay," said Sam, "just leave them there. I'll get to them eventually."

Man, he was really down.

"Listen, Sam, all of us wanted to thank you for saving the world. You did a real good thing last week."

"I know," said Sam. He didn't sound any happier.

"How's your head feel?" I asked.

"What?" said Sam.

"Your head, after you pushed over Grobar's factory. You must have some huge headache."

"No, no, my head's fine," said Sam.

"What about your stomach?" I asked.

"My stomach?"

"Yeah? After you ate all those lab notes the drug lords wanted, you must have some terrible cramps."

"No, my stomach's fine," answered Sam.

He sure wasn't his normal self. You might be wondering how Sam ended up in the Zoo. Well, as you know, he knocked over a building and the police didn't like that much. So they arrested him. They insisted that a destructive elephant had to be in the Zoo – or worse. My mom and I tried to work something out, but we failed. They were going to stick him behind bars, no matter what we did.

It was nice to know Sam's head and stomach were fine, but I expected that. Elephants have hard heads and tough stomachs. If they can eat trees, a few lab notes won't slow them down.

"Sam?" I asked.

"What?" replied Sam.

"Sam, what exactly is wrong?" Now I knew what was wrong, but I wanted him to tell me.

"I'm stuck in the Zoo, Eddy. You know I don't like zoos. I wanted to escape and I wanted to build my elephant city and I wanted to run around and have fun. But they caught me and they stuck me back in here. That's what's wrong. I'm going to spend my whole life in this Zoo."

At least I'd finally gotten more than a few words out of Sam.

"Sam?" I asked.

"Yes?" said Sam, a little annoyed, but at least a little happy I was talking to him.

"What makes you think you're going to spend your whole life in the Zoo?"

"I just will, Eddy, I know it. I'm too big to escape without anybody noticing me. I escaped once, I gave it my best shot, and I failed. What am I supposed to do?"

I didn't know elephants could get *that* depressed. "Come on, Sam, don't get so down."

"Why shouldn't I?" my giant friend asked.

"Because you will get out of here and you will build your elephant city."

"Yeah, right," said Sam. He obviously didn't believe me.

"Right is right!" I said. "All of your friends are pulling for you. Me and 'The Source' and Thursday and even my mom. All of us are here to help you get out. We're not going to be stopped by some bars at the Zoo." I had to say 'The Source' and not Bartholomew because my mom was there and she wasn't allowed to know Bartholomew's name.

"I guess you're right," said Sam, his voice picking up a bit.

"All of us need you to do one thing."

"What's that?" asked Sam, beginning to actually get interested in the conversation.

155

"We need you to be optimistic." I insisted. "It's hard to rescue a happy elephant; it might just be impossible to rescue a really depressed one."

"I guess I can do that," said Sam, perking up a little bit more.

"Now," I said, "I've got some nuts, Brazil Nuts. Thursday said you wanted some. Would you like them?"

Sam only thought for a moment. Then, just like that, he lifted his massive frame off the floor of his pen and trumbled over to me. One by one, Sam ate all the nuts. Slowly, a bigger and bigger smile grew on his face.

Once he was done he looked down at me and said, "It'll be alright, won't it, Eddy?"

I knew what my mom always said when I asked her that same question. So I gave Sam the same answer, "Sam, everything will be just fine."

We talked some more. I promised to visit every day and Sam told me to buy a season ticket to the Zoo. He was trying to be funny. Finally, my mom and I left.

Just before we got in our car, I thought about my dad. I don't know why, it just came out of the blue. I missed him just like I missed Sam and he was also locked away somewhere – although nobody knew where.

I wished he could come home.

Somehow, my mom knew what I was thinking.

She got down on her knees in the parking lot (her skirt got all dirty) and she gave me a giant hug. Then she said, "Eddy, everything will be just fine."

I hugged her back and just then, I knew that it was true.

We got into the car together and drove home.

Turn the page for more

Almost there

Kinda leaves you hanging, doesn't it?

I hate when books do that. But the fact is, if you want to find out what happens to my dad and what's going to happen with Sam, you're gonna need to read the next book.

Sorry, I know it's annoying.

I'll tell you a bit about the next book, if you'd like. Basically, there's this neurotic gopher named Squiggles – and she's off to cause some serious trouble for surface dwellers like you and me. We didn't know much about her plot until a squadron of rodent special forces attacked my mom's house.

Want to learn more? Turn the page to read chapter one of *Squiggles and the Pit of Destruction* and then visit **www.ShortEddy.com** to learn when you can get your hands on your own copy!

It'll be coming out in 2006!

The Apocalypse

"EVERYTHING MUST BE FILED PROPERLY!"

The voice was shrill, loud, mean and extremely unhappy. The voice belonged to Squiggles, one of the shrillest, loudest, meanest and least happy beings on the planet earth. She was also a gopher.

When Squiggles was in a mood like this, which was almost always, it was best to be somewhere else.

There were a few unfortunate folk who tended to hang out with Squiggles. They didn't really choose to hang out with her; they were paid to hang out with her. You see, they were her office staff.

When Squiggles let out her yell, they all scampered for the safety of their desks. More than anything else, they wanted to look busy.

But, while Squiggles was shrill, loud, mean and unhappy, she was not stupid. A file had been misplaced, and due to her superb sense of detail and organization it was only a matter of time before she figured out exactly who had misplaced it.

You might ask, 'what had been misplaced?' After all, you could say, 'The way Squiggles was acting, it must have been important. Maybe it was intimately connected with the future of the planet Earth.' If you were talking about any normal person you would have been right, but we're talking about Squiggles. In reality, the missing file wasn't important at all. It was just a file used to track the number of worms consumed by one of Squiggles' many task forces.

And even though the file had gone missing, it wasn't like Squiggles didn't know exactly what it said. Squiggles could have told you how many worms were consumed. That wasn't the point. The point was that "everything must be filed properly." Everything had to be organized perfectly. Squiggles had one real drive in life. She wanted the world outside of her head to be just as organized as the world inside her head. That wouldn't have really mattered, except that Squiggles wasn't just another neat freak. No, Squiggles had a few other things going for her. She was incredibly brilliant; she was incredibly driven, and she was incredibly ruthless.

All in all, she was an extremely dangerous gopher who just happened to be named Squiggles.

While Squiggles' brain meticulously worked out who had been working on which files, the guilty party, who went by the name of Wangle, sat at her desk working feverishly. Perhaps she thought that by completing a week of work in five minutes, she might be spared some of Squiggles' wrath.

Deep down, Wangle knew better. Wangle had been working for Squiggles for years by then and she knew her about as well as anybody did. Wangle had survived for that long by being quiet, by anticipating even Squiggles' most random whims and most of all, by not screwing up. Even as she worked madly to lessen Squiggles' wrath, she cursed herself for her carelessness.

For her part, Squiggles was looking forward to finding, and punishing, the guilty clerk. Such moments provided her with the little joy she found in her daily life. However, while proper filing was incredibly important, certainly more important than the well-being of one clerk, Squiggles mind was on another topic. Squiggles was *really* thinking about an entirely different file. And it was a file that only Squiggles had access to. It was a top secret file which she protected like nothing else.

2

The top secret file folder was dark red with a green band running from one corner to the other. As all of the clerks could have told you, red-tinted folders were closely associated with a project known by only one word, APOCALYPSE. And, as any clerk could have told you, the dark red folders with green bands running diagonally across them were perhaps the most important type of folder they kept. Those folders were the primary planning folders for APOCALYPSE. Squiggles thought about them quite a bit.

You see, APOCALYPSE was to be the culmination of her career. It was to be the point at which the world fell into Squiggles' lap and would finally benefit from her genius.

While most of Squiggles' brilliant mind was on the APOCA-LYPSE, she hadn't forgotten about the misplaced worm file. In due course, naturally, Squiggles determined that Wangle was the clerk who had misplaced the worm file. Squiggles walked to Wangle's desk, and stared down at her. Cornered, Wangle broke down. She pleaded, begged and cried for forgiveness. She insisted that her mistake would never be repeated. By that was not enough for Squiggles. Mistakes, even minor one-time mistakes, simply could not be tolerated. Wangle was fired and sentenced to five minutes of the world's most excruciating torture.

As Wangle's screams filled the room, as a lesson for the other clerks, Squiggles' thoughts returned to APOCALYPSE. There were only four dark red folders with green bands. Three of them contained parts of the plan that had already been implemented.

Only the fourth remained unimplemented.

As she stood there, listening to Wangle being tortured, Squiggles reviewed that last folder in her mind.

While the contents of that folder were awe inspiring, Squiggles liked the title most of all. The folder was titled, "Gopher's Revenge." It summed up, in two short words, a lifetime of struggle and a dream that was nearing realization.

3

You see, Squiggles was the head, heart and soul of MRN, the world's largest underground organization. Its full name was The Squigglistic Organization for the Organization of Planet Earth Along Rational Lines. As you might guess from the name, it was an organization she had built. And it was an organization devoted to only one cause:

The destruction of mankind.

However, while Squiggles dreamed of setting the world completely straight, she was a practical gopher. In the short-term, she knew she could only hope to fix the greatest of faults. In Squiggles' mind, the single greatest fault in the order of the world was that gophers lived underground while humans lived above the ground. It was a situation that would have to remedied.

Wangle dropped to the floor. She had been almost completely shattered by the five minutes of tickling she had endured.

Meanwhile, Squiggles had thought happy thoughts – thoughts of revenge and death and destruction.

APOCALYPSE was near.

Be Sure to Visit
www.ShortEddy.com